The HAMMER
that drove the
NAILS

The story of the man

The HAND

who crucified Jesus

that drove the

NAILS

J. FLETCHER RAY

CHRISTIAN ART PUBLISHERS

Published in South Africa by Christian Art Publishers
PO Box 1599, Vereeniging, 1930

© 2002

Cover designed by CHRISTIAN ART PUBLISHERS

Scripture taken and adapted from the *Holy Bible,* New International Version®. NIV®. Copyright © 1973, 1978, 1984, by International Bible Society. Used by permission of Zondervan Publishing House. All rights reserved.

Set in 12 on 14 pt Weidemann Book by Christian Art Publishers

Printed and bound by Creda Communications

ISBN 1-86852-885-5

© All rights reserved. No part of this book may be reproduced in any form without permission in writing from the publisher, except in the case of brief quotations in critical articles or reviews.

02 03 04 05 06 07 08 09 10 11 – 11 10 9 8 7 6 5 4 3 2

TABLE OF CONTENTS

	Introduction	7
1.	Pilate's Carpenters	13
2.	The Magician from Galilee	18
3.	Deborah and the Nazarene	21
4.	Bartimaeus Can See	25
5.	The Long-awaited Messiah?	31
6.	The Shepherd's Tale	35
7.	"For Unto Us a Child is Born"	45
8.	Prophet of Love	58
9.	The Nazarene Finds a Young Champion	63
10.	The Hour and the Power of Darkness	67
11.	"What Is Truth?"	77
12.	The Fatal Choice	82
13.	The Hand of a Child	92
14.	"They Do Not Know What They Are Doing"	99
15.	A Wanderer in the Night	110
16.	Hermas Goes Home	118
17.	The Third Day	128
18.	"The Resurrection and the Life"	142
19.	Joseph Gives a Funeral Oration	147
20.	Mary Magdalene Speaks	155
21.	"If Your Right Hand Causes You to Sin ..."	163
22.	The Snake Has Struck	167
23.	Scipio Leaves the Legion	171
24.	The Hero of the Mountain	178
25.	Twenty Years Later	187
	Addendum by Joseph of Arimathea	191

Introduction

The story I wish to relate here, about a great discovery made years ago, is so extraordinary and astonishing that I am compelled to beg the reader's pardon for the following personal remarks.

My interest in the Greek and Aramaic languages arose during my studies at university. Although I was preparing myself for one of the professions, my happiest hours were those spent in the library after each day's lectures, just browsing through the multitude of documents that were available at the university in these languages. Under the mentorship of my professor (whose enthusiasm for anything related to the former glory of ancient Greece was highly contagious), my knowledge increased rapidly; and by the time I had completed my professional studies and received my degree, I had a thorough knowledge of Greek and Aramaic.

In 1916, during World War I, I was stationed at the Italian front. In my wildest dreams I could not have known that I would encounter something in Italy that would be the turning point in my life, and which may very well be regarded as the greatest revelation received by mankind in two thousand years.

I was struck by a stray bullet, and the resulting wound did not heal quickly. I was therefore sent to Rome for further treatment. During the time of my recovery, I spent countless hours in the public buildings housing the ancient books and manuscripts of that city. In the process I attracted the attention of an old caretaker by the name of Guiseppe, who visited me one day. He wanted to know whether I would be interested in buying a small wooden box containing ancient documents. In his opinion the documents were very important, but the authorities had rejected them for inclusion in the archives, due to a lack of space. I had no intention of being swindled, but it did appear to me that this could be a valuable "find" that had escaped attention. Therefore I requested more information and since the answers seemed satisfactory, I took possession of the box and entrusted it to the care of a friend in the city until such time as I could leave Italy.

I found this Guiseppe a fascinating character. In fact, there was a mutual affection. He was descended from an ancient Roman family. "Not from the nobility," he answered my question, "nor rich. But we have our tradition." I sensed that there was something mysterious about him and that he wanted to share some kind of revelation. I cannot say for certain whether he knew anything about the contents of the box, but judging from his mysterious and confidential behaviour, I would venture to say that he did, because he was extremely anxious for me to take possession of the object. His parting words to me were: "I am the last descendant of an ancient race."

After the war I brought the box home with me, and, as is to be expected, I was anxious to investigate the contents. So it came to pass, one evening in June 1920, that I found myself facing the table on which the object of my curiosity stood. With a feeling of reverence I opened the box and broke the seals of the documents. When I finally saw scroll upon scroll of parchment, all still in very good condition, I had the sensation that I was in the presence of something mysterious. Judging from the sharp aroma that rose from the box, some form of preservative had been used.

I trembled with excitement that I tried in vain to suppress. I removed the scrolls and carefully probed the bottom of the box. There I found a long, thick nail, crimson and dulled by rust. Once again my hand explored, until – with a cry of horror – I withdrew the dark, stained bones of a human hand! I emptied the box. It contained two more nails, as well as the remainder of the full number of bones of a man's right hand, amputated at the wrist. I was surprised at the immense size of the bones; their original owner truly must have been a giant!

There was one more object: a small scrap of papyrus. At first I could not make out anything on it, but when I held it up to the lamp, I could decipher the following:

*Ἔφη ὁ Ἰησοῦς, Εἰή δεξιά σου Χείρ
σκανδαλίζει σε, ἔκκοψον αὐτήν*[1]

I studied the documents. Most of them were written in an awkward hand and, in my judgement, dated from the earliest years of the Christian era. There were other documents in another hand and in varying conditions of preservation. But more about this later.[2]

That night I scrutinised parts of the older writings. Only when the light of dawn started glimmering through the curtains, did I realise how the hours had flown past, and it was with a sense of regret that I put down the documents and retired to my room. Still, I was too excited to sleep, because the documents I had in my possession were the confessions of Scipio Martialis, *none other than the executioner who had crucified Christ.*

I devoted years to the translation of the confessions of Scipio, which proved to be a surprisingly difficult task. The translation presented in this book is not intended for the learned, but for the common reader, because Scipio's confessions are of such general importance that it would be a pity to limit them to a relatively small group of scholars. The translation is therefore more in the spirit than in the letter.

From part of one scroll, which might have been the diary of a soldier, and which was extremely difficult to decipher due to its state of decay, I discovered that Marcus Martialis, the father of Scipio, lived on the banks of the Tiber, and that he was an influential man, highly regarded for his learning. He was devastated when his son, Scipio, left the schools of learning and decided to enlist in the army of Tiberius as an ordinary soldier. It would also appear that there was an amorous adventure, probably unbeknown to the father, which drove the son to leave his home for foreign shores in an attempt to forget. More than this, I could not glean from the scanty record.

Almost two thousand years have passed. Kingdoms have risen and fallen; empires have come and gone. The might of Rome is now nothing more than the ghost of a passing dream. The members of the Sanhedrin, who walked the temple courts so haughtily have been gathered to their fathers, and the place of their dwelling knows them no more. But he whom they scorned and crucified is not forgotten. The Name of the Prince of Peace is written in blood across the pages of history.

Footnotes
1. Jesus said: *"... if your right hand causes you to sin, cut it off..."* (Mt. 5:30).
2. One document, entitled "The Garden of the Grave", relates the fascinating experiences of Scipio over a period of twenty years as gardener in the service of Joseph of Arimathea. Perhaps this will be published later. When *"The Hand That Drove The Nails"* first had to be published in English, we addressed the following question to the author: "May we be so bold as to ask whether the introduction to the book was written only to enhance the value of the book, or whether the documents you refer to are actually in your possession?"

We received the following reply: "In 1917, while I was in active military service during World War I, I was billeted with a certain Bruna Martialis, one of the most devout people I ever had the honour to know. Together we spent hours poring over his Greek New Testament. He was a hermit and it took me a while to gain his confidence. Only after I had succeeded in this, did he confide in me that he was the only living descendant of Scipio Martialis – the man who crucified our Lord Jesus. He showed me documented proof on condition that I would keep it to myself.

"Later he described the wooden box and its contents to me and also told me that he had the box in safekeeping in Tuscany. (I understood that it was buried somewhere.) In the days that followed we spoke of nothing else.

"After the war we would travel to Italy, recover the treasure and reveal its tale to the world. But, unfortunately, this was not to be.

"One day, towards the end of 1917, I left the trenches for a few hours. Upon my return I discovered that a direct hit by a bomb had wiped out the life and identity of my dear friend, as well as everything that belonged to him! This, in brief, is the story. Consequently, I have neither the wooden box nor the documents in my possession.

"Upon my return to England a tragic misfortune befell me. Through the long months of despair that followed, I kept these things to myself, but eventually I divulged my story to certain literary scholars and they advised me to write the introduction as if I were actually in possession of the box and its contents."

— *The Publisher* —

Chapter 1

Pilate's carpenters

(The writings of Scipio Martialis, soldier of the legion of the army of Emperor Tiberius, stationed in Jerusalem in the time of our Lord Jesus Christ.)

My legion was based to the east of the Sea of Galilee, in the hills above Gadara.

Our presence was the consequence of an uprising among the Galileans. The struggle continued for some time outside the town of Sefforis and there were many casualties. One day, while we were pursuing the Galileans far from the battlefield, nightfall overcame us. I was trying to find my way back to camp in the darkness, when I suddenly stumbled over something and fell to the ground. A band of Galileans, who had sought shelter in the adjacent woods, overpowered me before I could get up and onto my feet. They viciously assaulted me and left me for dead.

I do not recall what happened next, but when I finally opened my eyes, I was lying in some kind of a cave, while skilled hands were dressing my wounds. "Even though you are a Roman," I heard a soft voice whisper, "and although you are an enemy of Israel, I cannot allow you to die here."

It was the voice of a Jewish girl, Susanna. (I could understand her, although she was speaking in Aramaic.) For days she braved grave danger to bring me food and water. One day she told me that her mother was dying, and that her father had been taken to Caesarea as a prisoner, together with many others, there to be sold as a slave.

My wounds were tended to in a very competent manner. Since I was strong and fit, I quickly regained my strength. When I rejoined the legion, I was resolved to marry no-one but Susanna. After many days we were united in marriage, for Licinius had awarded special permission to the Jewish girl who had saved and nursed a Roman soldier back to health.

Shortly after my lord Pilate came to Jerusalem as plenipotentiary, I had the honour of protecting him when he fell into the hands of thieves while on an unaccompanied secret mission one dark night. I was passing the spot by chance. Because of this, the governor instructed Licinius, the centurion, to furnish a private dwelling for me approximately half a mile from the Antonia Fortress. I was delighted because Susanna had already made me the proud father of a daughter, Nidia, and a son, whom I had named Hermas.

I was also relieved from my duty of standing guard on the ramparts, unless special circumstances required it. The Antonia Fortress was on the western hill of Jerusalem. It covered a large area of Mount Moriah, opposite the Mount of Olives, and controlled the colonnades of the temple. It was made up of armouries, warehouses, barracks, workshops and jail cells.

My lord Pilate had been governor here for three years, succeeding Valerius Gratus. His palace was adjacent to the tower. It was my job to do any kind of carpentry required in and around the palace. And so it often came to pass that I did odd jobs for my lord Pilate and his wife, the noble Claudia Procula.

From the ramparts we had a view of the palace of Antipas. We intensely disliked Herod Antipas. He was cruel and selfish and still intent on waging war. His capital was Tiberias. Those of us who served under him thought little of him as a leader or as a person.

The seven of us who served under Licinius were relieved of many of the duties in the legion because we worked in the joinery in the courtyard. We repaired the battering rams, chariots and transport wagons. Sometimes we felled trees and selected the best ones to make crucifixes, because our duties also included the execution of criminals. We found this a welcome change from the garrison duties and long journeys, although there were times when we had to exchange the axe for the sword and march to suppress some or other small uprising in the vicinity. It was evident that these expeditions were not regarded favourably by the Jews. Sour faces and curses were the only greetings we received from the stubborn dogs – and if a soldier had the audacity to leave his comrades and camp alone in the field, he would be lucky to return to the garrison unscathed. Yes, those were times of unrest!

As I have already mentioned, there were seven of us, as well as a number of slaves, involved in the carpenter's trade. In spite of the fact that we complained at times, we were very satisfied with the work, since it allowed us to escape many troublesome duties and gave us a measure of freedom that few soldiers were entitled to. After the reparations had been completed, we sat in the sun many long hours, drinking and gambling and talking about women, or sports, or war; or sometimes about our childhood days, our families, our countries of birth. At other times we went to the courtyard to wrestle, fence with swords, or throw the discus.

There were not many who could persevere against us. Quintus was the best swordsman among us. He was tall and lean, but also as fleet-footed as a cat and as straight as a reed. Quintus the Silent, we called him. He listened a lot, but said very little. He was quiet and gentle in nature, but did not know the meaning of fear. His thin face, covered with scars, was as pointy as an axe, and as brown as that of a son of Egypt. His friends teased him a great deal, because he did not sleep with any other woman but his wife.

Caius Antonius served under me. His face was red and his eyes blue, and he was very proud of his full black beard, which gave him an exceptionally stern appearance. He was a fierce fighter, and also reckless and daring. Yet, he had no special skills. He could laugh his head off at mere trifles. I was quite fond of him because he worked hard and had more pride than vice.

Rufus was like a brother to me. No one was his equal at wrestling. His skin was as pale as that of a woman; his hair and beard were red. He was fun-loving and always full of jokes, carefree as the sparrows, and witty too. He hardly ever complained, and he always sang while he worked, like the birds. Hardly a day passed without him losing his saw, or his axe, or his plane. His father was a learned man, but Rufus had no love for the senate or the council chambers and sought freedom and danger in the army. This in no way suggests that he was mentally slow. His conversations attested to his intelligence – and sometimes also to his great learning, because he possessed a wealth of knowledge about Greek art and literature. Many of the songs he sang were the product of his own ingenuity; and his heart was no smaller than his bulky form. I had witnessed him crying like a baby for someone else's loss, and had seen him giving his last penny to a fellow soldier. We often talked about the joyful wedding celebration we had when he married a woman by the name of Deborah. She hailed from the Plain of Sharon and was as beautiful as the rose that bloomed there.

I didn't like Probus at all. He was a giant of a man. In fact, he was only four centimetres shorter than I. But he loved the sound of his own voice, which usually uttered more filth than sense. He loved feasting, drinking and wanton women, to the extent that he sometimes became an embarrassment, even to the soldiers who usually forgave many misdemeanours. He quarrelled with everyone, as is usually the case with someone who is exceedingly strong. Nevertheless, his excessive life had undermined his masculinity to such an extent that I could easily throw him.

The other two carpenters came from Capernaum; Varus and Hamon were their names. I took them in at the workbench, because they had served under old Marcus Secundus, the centurion under whom I had also served as an adolescent. They spent a lot of their time with the women of the city and then shared the gossip of the marketplace with us, in spite of the fact that we were not in the least interested, except for Probus, who took great pleasure in these tales.

As for me, they called me Scipio the Bull, because I had at one time participated in the bullfights in the arena in Rome. I was of enormous build, and it was said that I did not know the extent of my own strength.

Our little group in the carpenter's trade travelled a great deal and served in Italy, Greece, Egypt, Iberia and Gaul. Consequently we were never at a loss for conversation, and we talked a lot about the wonderful things that we had witnessed and the adventures we had experienced. Not one of us was without some scar inflicted by sword or spear. We told many wonderful tales about bloody battles fought in distant lands. In the midst of the peaceful life we led with our comrades, Rufus and I had no way of knowing that a day would arrive when we would be thankful for the measure of learning that we had. For this thing, that was forced upon us in our youth, was destined to strengthen the bond of camaraderie between us.

Chapter 2

The magician from Galilee

Jerusalem was teeming with interesting things, such as soldiers swaggering down the narrow streets and clanking chariots forging ahead through the crowded main streets. I have always been fascinated by the places where people gather and by their conversations about things that had happened in distant countries.

I doubt whether there is another city anywhere in the world with a history as strange as that of the capital city of Judea. Here one can see the temple built by Solomon; the seven kilometres of city wall with its watchtowers; Pilate's huge aqueduct, twenty-five kilometres of solid rock; the palaces of Pontius Pilate and Herod; the house of Caiaphas; Mount Zion, and the Mount of Olives. I had no way of knowing then, as I sat in the shade of the olive trees one evening, that the city in front of me would one day cast a shadow over my life.

Sometimes I ventured onto the winding stone roads and walked among the people who spoke in strange tongues. I watched as camels, donkeys, oxen and goats were chased aside to make way for the chariots of war or for the soldiers of the legion, who marched past, dressed in their breastplates and helmets.

From the workshop we could look down upon the temple, and we often stood there and watched the priests come and go, as well as the teachers of the law, the Sadducees and the Pharisees, who were rumoured to be about six thousand in number. It was easy to distinguish them because they wore broad phylacteries and always tried to draw attention to themselves in public places. They often stood in the streets, praying out loud so that they would be heard by the people. They were a callous, self-righteous bunch, and we returned their greetings reluctantly when we encountered them in the narrow streets. They made their way through the crowds with downcast eyes, or raised their hands and invoked Jehovah at the top of their voices in public places. The poor, the crippled and the maimed humbly stood aside to allow these men to pass. The sheep did not have much love for their shepherds!

"Greed! Wealth! Blackmail! Pride!" was the summary of a beggar outside the temple gates, when they walked past him without even noticing his existence. He was lucky that his words did not reach any ears other than mine. Although they were callous and cold, they were also quick-tempered. On countless occasions I was commandeered to join the detachment of soldiers sent to quell an uprising and prevent bloodshed between the Jews and the Samaritans. For there was discord among them, and I knew who the instigators were.

How well I remember the day Varus and Hamon joined our group from Capernaum. Varus wanted to know whether we had heard about a man called Jesus of Nazareth, a prophet whom (so he said) the entire Capernaum followed. "And they say," Hamon added, "that he healed many people who had been gravely ill. Yes," and here he lowered his voice, "someone in Korazin told me that he touched a man called Josiah who had been a leper for many years, and immediately he was completely healed."

"Yes," Varus said, "He is the one to whom Marcus Secundus – you know him, Scipio, for you served under him – sent his slave with the request that the healer must heal his dear servant who was dying."

"By the gods!" Probus said. "It must be the magician who attended the wedding in Cana. I heard about him; and also how, when the wineskins were empty, he took water and turned it into wine. And by all the gods, I wish we had that magician with us now, because we have lots of water here, but very little wine!"

Everybody laughed heartily, and after Quintus went to fetch a bag of wine, we put down our tools and feasted. When the bag was empty, Hamon filled it from the well and we prayed to the gods to send us such a prophet to turn water into wine. And that, as far as I can remember, was the first time I heard about the Galilean. We carried on drinking until the break of day. Little did we know, during that night of drunkenness, that the fate of that man from Galilee would become so closely intertwined with our own.

Chapter 3

Deborah and the Nazarene

We often received visitors in the workshop. During the heat of the day we usually sat drinking wine, exchanging the gossip of the Praetorium and the marketplace. One of our most frequent visitors was a man by the name of Bartimaeus, who had been born blind. He habitually begged at the temple gates. Rufus had come across him one day just as a Pharisee was abusing him, and because of his big heart, he protected the poor fellow. Consequently, Bartimaeus loved Rufus as a child loves his father, and Rufus, although very proud, had a high regard for the wisdom of the blind man, and once in a while gave him part of his rations, or slipped a denarius to him.

So it came to pass that, as soon as we heard the sound of a walking stick on the paving, we knew that Bartimaeus was approaching. His arrival was always accompanied by the flapping of wings around him, because the birds loved Bartimaeus, and so did the little children.

When my son Hermas was with me, his face would light up with joy when he saw the blind man approaching. Then he would lead him around the workshop and have him touch the battering rams, transport wagons and chariots sent to us for repairs. On these occasions Hermas would dress up in the helmet, breastplate and sword that Rufus had made for him, and with outstretched sword he would give orders. I was always very pleased about this, because I was proud of my son, and my heart's desire was that he would one day lead his own men into war. Rufus and Quintus were very fond of him, because they loved children. They played with him and laughed at his pranks and witty banter, because, although he was only nine years old, he was wise beyond his years. He was also a favourite among the men of the garrison.

In the course of time many people visited us, while some in our group also visited the bazaars. In this way we came to know quite a bit about that Galilean. We were told that his name was on everyone's lips. Some told of the powerful deeds that he performed in Galilee, while others assured us that he would even come to Jerusalem one day. Some spoke of the days when they had seen him in the streets of the city with their own eyes.

There were rumours that he had evoked the wrath of the temple leaders, and that they had sent some of the cleverest teachers of the law and Pharisees to entrap him with trick questions. It was also no secret that they were secretly plotting to kill him.

"Another magician," Probus said one day when he had had enough of all this talk in the workshop. "By Jupiter! Have you all gone mad? Why do you listen to the tales of vagabonds? Has there ever been someone who could heal a leper simply by touching him, or who could open the eyes of a blind man? One of these days you will ask me to believe that he has woken the dead. Isn't it enough that you laze around? Must you tell lies too, and deal in foolish talk?" Since he was slightly drunk and had also managed to cut his finger, he started yelling at us.

"Look here, Probus, you fool, plug your ears if you do not wish to hear these things. Leave us in peace and go and look at your mug in a clear stream, then your foul tongue will stop spouting obscenities at us." These were my words, not that I troubled myself with the actions of this Nazarene, but I was angry at the drunk Probus for making such a racket. However, the wine had gone to his head, and in response to my words his hand immediately went to his sword, but I grabbed his arm and with a move that I had been taught by old Casca, the swordsman, I threw him on his back. I did not tolerate abuse from anyone.

He slowly rose to his feet. Perhaps he remembered our last tussle, because with a sidelong glance in my direction, he sullenly returned to his work. But do not think that I scolded Probus for love of this Galilean. No, in truth my heart was hardened towards him. I did not pay much attention to the talk of the marketplace, and I did not believe any of the wonderful things said about him. There are many prophets among the gullible. Only a few months earlier everyone had been talking about a man called John, who baptised people, but now he had already been forgotten. However, to tell the truth, I was slightly worried about some of the things that were being said, namely that this man called himself a king, with the same measure of authority as my lord Pilate himself, and that he would invade Jerusalem with an army. I was no longer a young man and was tired of bloodshed.

I still remember clearly that this was my train of thought as I was on my way to the workshop one day. It was still rather early, but Quintus the Silent was already there when I arrived. I could see in his eyes that something had touched him deeply.

"Have you heard?" he asked.

"What now?" I asked.

"The Pharisees," he answered, "took a woman to the Nazarene, a woman who had been caught in the act of adultery. They read to him from the law of their Moses which stipulates that such a woman had to be stoned. The woman hid her face in shame and fear, while the Pharisees and the crowd were shouting their accusations: 'The law says that she must die, but what do you say?' The Nazarene kneeled and wrote with his finger in the dust, but did not say a word. They then started crowding in upon him; and they watched the writing finger; but no one knew what he was writing. 'Blood!' they shouted. 'The blood of the adulteress! Moses gives us her blood!'

"Then the Nazarene rose to his feet. He held up his hand and everybody fell silent. He looked every man in the eye one by one. Nobody made a sound. Then he addressed them." For a moment

Quintus paused before he resumed slowly, "'If any one of you is without sin, let him be the first to throw a stone at her.' The crowd remained silent as the grave, and then there was a restless movement. One of those on whom he fixed his gaze dropped his stone and turned pale, as pale as a leper. One after the other they dropped the stones, one by one. And as he looked at them, they dispersed, pale and ashen and trembling. No one remained. Then he went and kneeled beside the woman and asked, 'Woman, where are your accusers? Has no one condemned you?' Then the woman looked around her and answered, 'Not one, Sir.'

"And what do you think happened next, Scipio? Tenderly the Nazarene looked at the kneeling woman and said to her, 'I don't condemn you either. Go now and leave your life of sin.'

"With tears of joy about her new-found absolution, the woman left him alone in the temple court."

Quintus was silent and looked at me. My eyes met those serious, calm eyes. "Carry on, Quintus," I said. "Carry on, because I can see there is more."

He looked me straight in the eye. "That woman was none other than Deborah, the wife of Rufus!"

And so it came about that from that day onwards, no one dared say a word about the Nazarene whenever Rufus was in the vicinity. He became quiet and reserved, so that no one dared speak to him. And when he spoke about the priests and Pharisees, he spoke with a bitterness I had never heard in him before. He guarded the things this prophet had said in his heart and never discussed it with anyone, except with Bartimaeus.

Chapter 4

Bartimaeus can see

One evening, while we were busy with repairs on the transport wagons in the workshop someone that we took for a lunatic, wrenched open the door. He was surrounded by flapping birds and a swarm of children followed him. Although he was out of breath from running, he shouted loudly, "Scipio! Rufus! Caius! Probus! All you Romans! Look! My eyes are open! I can see! I can see!"

And truly, it was none other than the blind Bartimaeus – but no longer blind! He could not tell us apart until he had heard our voices, or had touched us as he used to do. We were so astonished that it was a while before we noticed the rabble that had accompanied him, although it was forbidden to meet in the courtyard. We had no idea how they had managed to get past the guards. Only later did we hear that the guards were so surprised that Bartimaeus was no longer blind, that they simply forgot their duty.

We questioned him closely about the way in which he was healed, but before he could answer, he first quenched his thirst, while we drove off the mob that had followed him. He had rushed all the way from Jericho to see us. After a short rest, he told us how his eyes had been opened.

He was begging by the roadside (so he told us) when he heard a large crowd approaching. Some of the people at the forefront told him that the Galilean was about to pass by that spot. Upon hearing this news he shouted loudly, "Son of David, Jesus, have mercy on me!" Hereupon Jesus came to a halt and sent for him; and he touched his eyes and enabled him to see.

We were speechless with astonishment on hearing this account, except for Probus, who cursed and swore by all the gods that we were idiots and fools. "He was never blind," Probus said. "This man has deceived all of you, so that he could eat the bread of an idle vagabond." And with disgust he turned his back on us. But we paid him no heed and continued questioning Bartimaeus about his healing, upon which he answered us like before. "Furthermore," he continued, "I will no longer be a beggar, because I have a job in the house of a man called Zacchaeus."

"What!" Caius exclaimed. "You don't mean Zacchaeus the tax-collector? He who sold himself to Rome for the privilege of sucking his countrymen dry? By the gods! There is no man in Judea who is hated more by the Jews than this man. A robber of the poor! A devourer of households!"

"Yes, the same man," Bartimaeus answered, "and yet, *not the same man*. This Jesus also opened his eyes, and now he recognises his sins. This is what happened: when Jesus was about to enter Jericho, Zacchaeus, who is a very short man, climbed into a tree by the roadside to have a better view of the Nazarene, because he was surrounded by a huge crowd. Then Jesus said to him, 'Zacchaeus, come down immediately. I must stay at your house today.' Everyone was dumbfounded, because they knew how grave a sinner he was.

"And now, since he has seen this prophet, everything has changed. And I, Bartimaeus, who used to sit at the gates begging, have a large sum of money with me right now, as well as a list of names of those people who were wronged by Zacchaeus. A man by the name of Reuben from Jericho will read the names to me, and regarding the money, I know the coins by touch. Zacchaeus took an oath to give half of his possessions to the poor, and if he extorted money from someone, he will repay them fourfold. And so I have come to Jerusalem to bring reparation to the people whose names I have here with me."

"By Jupiter!" Caius exclaimed. "That is a bigger miracle than the opening of your eyes, Bartimaeus, because I know this Zacchaeus well. We have done some business together." And he spat on the ground.

That night I took Bartimaeus out on the road to Bethany, since I wanted to know more. It was wonderful to see him marvel like a child at the things we encountered along the way. It was hard not to laugh as he asked me the names of the trees and the animals and the houses we saw. He told me that he sometimes had to close his eyes in Jerusalem to find his way. Everything was strange and new to him. Light and colour filled him with delight.

"Will you recognise the Galilean if you were to see him again?" I asked him.

"Yes, Scipio, among ten thousand; because his face was the first I ever saw." And then he added tenderly: "Whether I live or die, that face will always be before me."

When we arrived at the top of the Mount of Olives, we stopped. Jerusalem was spread out before us in the glow of the setting sun. The man who used to be blind stood there like one enchanted – speechless. And to me (perhaps because I was looking through his eyes), the city was more beautiful than ever before. The dome of the temple was like pure gold; the white rooftops were etched against the sapphire sky; and the tranquil hills and valleys were spread out in the glow of the changing light. A shepherd passed us with his sheep, carrying one little lamb in his arms.

"My Lord!" Bartimaeus exclaimed. "My Lord! How wonderful! How glorious!" He fell to the ground and kissed the grass and the flowers and sobbed out loud. "O Jesus!" he called. "Jesus, I thank you, I thank you!"

It would indeed have been a strange sight for any passer-by: a Roman soldier, with a short little man by his side who was acting like a lunatic. I took him by the hand and helped him to his feet. "Bartimaeus," I said, "look me in the eye and listen to me. You have lived in Jericho for a long time. To the west are the fields of

Moab and Ammon, and there a certain doctor called Amenophis lives, an Egyptian who performs wonderful healings. Yes, it is rumoured that he even gave eyes to those who were sitting in the dark. Bartimaeus, look me in the eye again and tell me the truth: was it not he who healed your eyes so that you can see? Did you lie to me about this Jesus of Nazareth?" And in my heart I was resolved that I would tear out his tongue if he had deceived me.

He looked at me and was overcome by an immense sadness. "Scipio," he said with tearful eyes, "Scipio, you always treated me with empathy when I was enveloped in darkness. I would never, I *could* never lie to you. What I have told you in the courtyard was nothing less than the truth. I visited this Amenophis years ago, but he could not do anything for me."

"But how is it possible that this Galilean, who is a man from the same trade as us, and without any training in these things – how could somebody like him heal your eyes?"

"Scipio, although you have always been my friend, I cannot answer your question. I know only this: I was blind, and now I can see."

I let it be and we continued walking. For a long time I did not say a word, because I was very confused and disturbed. The sun crept closer to the horizon as we approached Bethany.

"Have you ever heard about the man named Lazarus who lives here?" Bartimaeus asked me.

"Yes!" I replied. "Who hasn't heard the nonsense told about him? It was the talk of the marketplace. Is there anything you wouldn't believe?" For a while Bartimaeus was silent. We entered the town. There were beautiful orchards on both sides of the road that passed between the overhanging palm tress. Some women were drawing water at the town well, and Bartimaeus asked one of them where the house of Lazarus and his sisters Martha and Mary was. The woman showed him a low dwelling that was almost obscured by a number of fruit trees. It was a peaceful house some distance from the road, and there were no other houses in its immediate vicinity.

"Don't be angry, Scipio," Bartimaeus pleaded, "I want to ask him personally. Are you coming with me?"

"No, I will wait outside. But be quick!" He left me and I restlessly paced up and down under the palm trees. When he returned, his face was radiant with happiness, which just angered me more.

"Well," I asked, "did you see the dead man?"

"No," he replied, "Lazarus has left to go to Christ so that he can follow him."

"They'll tell that to everyone who comes here, believe me. Let's return before it gets dark," I said. In silence we set off in the direction of Jerusalem, Bartimaeus in front and I trailing behind a few feet. I cannot explain why I hardened my heart towards the Galilean. It was not as if I had any love for the priests who were his enemies. Yes, I did love Bartimaeus whom he had healed, and it grieved me to know that my words had hurt him. But Bartimaeus could not remain quiet for long. We had gone only a short distance when he started telling me what he had heard about Lazarus.

"Bartimaeus," I interrupted him, "shut up and listen to what I have to say. Years ago, when I was living in Rome, there was the controversial case of a certain Timon who lay like a dead man for twenty days. He did not stir, nor did he eat anything; and then, one day, he got up and walked. I saw him with my own eyes. That is probably what happened with this Lazarus too, if there is any truth in the story. And this man from Galilee boasts that he had raised him from the dead. Bartimaeus, you are no fool, why do you believe these things?"

He was quiet for a moment, and I knew that I had hurt him deeply. Then, with a voice trembling with emotion, he said, "Scipio, my dear friend, how can you doubt? Do you forget that I used to be blind?"

I bit my tongue and walked on in silence. My heart hardened towards him, because I could not think of a reply. But how empty my heart was, because I had always loved Bartimaeus deeply; and I was on my way to an empty house, because Susanna and my son had gone out of town for a number of days. When I arrived home I came to a standstill. I still remember how dark everything was because it was already late and the clouds hid the stars. He whom

I loved came to me and, as was his habit, put his hand on my shoulder.

"Farewell, Scipio," he said, "and peace be with you!" He was quiet as he prepared to leave; but then he turned back and once again put his hand on my shoulder. "Scipio," he begged, "please do not harden your heart towards me, because I love you deeply."

I did not answer him, but walked him to the door. Yet, before I opened it, I turned to him once more. Suddenly the moon shone through the clouds, and there I saw him in the moonlight, slender and weak, leaning with bowed head on his walking stick. A great longing filled my soul. The next moment I was by his side and put my arms around him. "Bartimaeus, friend of my heart! Take comfort, because tonight you will sleep under my roof. Come in!"

I turned hastily and went into the house, afraid that I might act like a woman, and he followed me inside.

Chapter 5

The long-awaited Messiah?

(Susanna, wife of Scipio Martialis, tells what came to pass and everything she had heard while tending to a woman called Rebecca of Bethlehem during the birth of her first child.)

When I learned the art of writing from Rabbi Isaac, I never thought that I would one day record such important things as I would like to tell of here.

It is fortunate that I have some knowledge of nursing, because a soldier does not earn a lot; and in these difficult times a denarius does not go very far. Consequently I often went to Jerusalem to take care of women during their delivery.

One day Darius, the shepherd, brought news to me that a certain Rebecca of Bethlehem was very near her time, and that she wanted me to tend to her. This Rebecca was very close to my heart, because, unlike other Jewish women who did not want to know me after I married Scipio, the Roman, her love became even stronger.

Therefore I left Nidia, my eldest daughter, at home to care for her father, and departed for Bethlehem with my nine-year old son, Hermas. We left home early in the morning. The journey was slow, because the road was crowded with oxen and donkeys and sheep and goats, as well as many people. Also, Hermas did not want to walk fast, but wanted to stop to look at the kneeling camels and their dark-skinned drivers from Nubia. He often took me by the hand and dragged me to the place where a group of women stood by their pitchers, commending their syrups and grape honey to passers-by. Sometimes he pressed up to me when some or other vagabond with a vicious face glared threateningly at us. I was impatient at these delays, and was very relieved when Flavius from the garrison, whom Hermas knew well, joined us and escorted us safely past a gang of tanned savages with long beards and dirty faces, who forced their way through the throng.

From there we headed for the Hinnom Valley, which is situated to the left of Mount Zion. We rested a while and had breakfast at the Pool of Solomon, before taking the road between the olive orchards to the Hill of Mar Elias, from where we could see Bethlehem across the valley.

"Have courage, my brave little boy!" I encouraged Hermas, because by that time he was exhausted. "There among the trees is Rebecca's house." As I spoke these words, Rebecca came towards us, and her joy at seeing us was clear.

She gave us water to wash our feet, and then we sat down under the leafy trees to enjoy our meal. Hermas was so tired that he fell asleep directly after we had eaten. The sun was already low, and Rebecca and I made ourselves comfortable under the olive trees to talk about the olden days.

"Have you heard about the prophet of Nazareth?" Rebecca finally asked.

"No," I replied, "I don't heed the gossip of the marketplace. Scipio has said some things about him, but not much. He says there is often talk of him in the workshop, for example about the fact that he calls himself a king – and that bodes bloodshed. Perhaps Scipio will have to fight too. Ah, Rebecca, you don't know what it's like to be the wife of a soldier!"

"No, Susanna," she replied, very pleased with herself for knowing more about the prophet than I did. "Look, you know very little about him. Perhaps you city people can still learn something from us country folk. Listen carefully!

"You have read the Scriptures, because you are a daughter of Israel, even if you are the wife of a Roman. And I'm sure you must have prayed for the coming of God's chosen One, the Christ; that he may come to break the chains binding Israel; because your heart is with the children of your faith, and your ears are not shut against their calls. Well, listen then!

"Do you remember John who baptised people in the River Jordan? Before he was thrown in jail, he spoke about someone who would come, whose sandals he was not fit to loosen, and who would save Israel. Susanna, this prophet from Galilee is the one John and the prophets spoke about. He is the Son of God. He came to restore the throne of David. And I saw him with my own eyes, Susanna, and perhaps you too will get to see him."

I looked up and stared at her intently, so that she fell quiet, although, to tell the truth, I wanted to know more. However, I did not want her to upset herself, because her time was near; so I took her to lie down on her bed.

I returned to the garden and sat under the trees for a long time with Hermas asleep in my lap, while I contemplated everything I had heard about the Nazarene. Although I was married to a Roman, my heart was with the children of the house of Israel; and I never served any other god but the God of my fathers. Since I had heard the teachings of John, by whom I had also been baptised (although I hid it carefully from Scipio), I had thought a lot about the Scriptures and the prophecies. But nobody had told me that this prophet from Galilee was the Holy one of God; the one who would lead Israel until his enemies would be crushed under his feet.

And my heart became heavy, because, if he were truly the Messiah, the might of Rome would be humiliated; and I was afraid for Scipio, because he knew no other law than the word of Pilate. He could even die in the battle. It could happen that the Messiah would not have mercy on him, even though he was the husband of a daughter of Israel who had always worshipped the God of her fathers!

I involuntarily clasped Hermas closer to my breast, so that he stirred in his sleep and mumbled, "Mommy!" Then he smiled and closed his eyes again. His face was pale in the approaching dusk.

Lights were beginning to shine in the houses of the workers everywhere. The evening shadows descended on a peaceful scene; the quiet was only disturbed by the lowing of cattle and the bleating of sheep. The stars looked down upon this wretched world of people and war and blood. It was so quiet that I could even hear the breathing of my child. I bowed my head and cried, and under my tears I prayed that this Christ would be someone with a gentle and compassionate heart; and that my husband would not be counted among those whose blood had to vindicate the suffering of Israel. Then I took Hermas in my arms and entered the quiet house.

Chapter 6

The shepherd's tale

When I awoke the next morning, the sun was already high in the sky, and the fear and doubts of the previous night had faded like the memories of a half-forgotten dream. I got up hastily and found Rebecca waiting for me. It was not long before she started talking about the Galilean again, the man (she said) the people called Jesus of Nazareth. She talked about nothing else. It appeared that her mother, Joanna, already an old woman, was the midwife who had tended to the mother when the child was born. Rebecca promised that she herself would tell me everything that had occurred *that* night.

Then Rebecca told me about old Isaac, a shepherd, who had heard the angels sing that night the child was born, and I had to leave with her immediately to meet this Isaac. The field where he herded his sheep was only a short distance away, and although I felt a little uneasy about her condition, she would not hear of postponing the visit. So we left and Rebecca made the journey pass quickly with stories about the miracles performed by this Jesus of Nazareth. Even Hermas, who disliked being in the company of grown-ups while they were talking, walked by her side and listened attentively to every word she said.

We were hardly out of town before we found ourselves among

the hills of Judea that separate Bethlehem from the great valleys. We rested underneath the wild fig trees next to the olive and mulberry orchards of Rabbi Ezra, and spoke about the lovely Ruth, from the distant Moab, who may have gathered ears of corn in those very fields where the waving corn was glistening in the morning sun. Hermas ran around picking the lilies of the field.

"May it please God to give me a boy, Susanna," Rebecca said with feeling, "then I will take him to this Jesus so that he may bless him." She lowered her head and cried in silence for a while. Then we got up and continued on our way.

Soon afterwards we arrived at the place where old Isaac was. He greeted Rebecca with joy, because he had known her for many years. He was very friendly and I liked him from the start. Although he was bent with age and full of wrinkles, he was as simple and friendly as a child, and lacked the loud arrogance and audacity of the people of the city. He immediately grew fond of Hermas. He listened with infinite patience to all his questions and admired his sturdy limbs, something that made me very proud. Hermas stroked the long white beard of the shepherd with his little fingers.

We had hardly finished our greetings before two boys arrived to help tending the herd. They had brought along a lamb whose mother had died. Isaac cradled it in his arms as a mother would hold her firstborn and fed it milk from a gourd. Hermas's eyes grew wide with astonishment, and he kept pleading also to hold the lamb. It gave old Isaac great pleasure to see the child play with the lamb in his arms. He showed the boy how they call sheep with the reed-pipe, and gave him the shepherd's crook to hold.

Rebecca asked the shepherd to tell me what had happened the night he had heard the angels sing. He first wanted to know more about me. "Not because I distrust you, child," he said, "but those in power have little love for the Master, and I therefore have to be careful."

He sat down on a fallen tree and gazed far out over the hillocks, as if he saw things there in the distance that were visible only to him. His eyes were pale blue and watery with old age; but when his gaze rested upon the hills, love and tenderness filled them with such a wonderful beauty that I was mesmerised.

"I remember everything so clearly," he said, "as if it happened only last night. It all took place one night approximately thirty-two years ago. I remember this, because we had slaughtered two of the sheep and took them to Cornelius, the innkeeper, because there were many strangers in Bethlehem that day who had come to register for the census.

"I am the only surviving shepherd of the three who tended the herds that night. Ephraim has been gathered to his fathers, and Daniel has gone to Galilee, or perhaps to Samaria – I'm not sure where – to see Christ.

"We sat here on the ground and watched the sheep, or huddled next to the fire that we had made to keep away the wild animals and we talked about many things. Exhausted, I later wrapped myself in my sheepskin and slept. Suddenly I was woken by Ephraim. His face was ashen in the glow of the fire. I grabbed my stick.

"'Isaac!' he called. 'Isaac, wake up and listen! Tell me, what do you hear?' I sat up and listened. Something stirred in the bushes, but quite far off. In the distance a jackal cried. The stars were brilliant and cold above us. Everything was quiet and peaceful.

"'Go to bed, Ephraim,' I said. 'Go to sleep. There's nothing.'

"'No, I cannot sleep,' he said. 'I heard it twice. No, sleep I cannot. Something wonderful is going to happen tonight, Isaac. I am very scared.'

"'What did you hear? Tell me!'

"'No, you will mock me. But I am certain that I heard it.' Suddenly he grabbed me by the arm. 'There it is again! Listen!'

"And I listened. Clear and beautiful the song of a bird travelled through the night, but it was much more beautiful than the song of any earthly bird. We listened, while we held each other. Daniel joined us. Suddenly the song stopped. We looked at one another, but no one said a word. And then ...

"'Look!' Daniel said in a strange and hoarse voice. 'Look!' Above that hill we saw it. It was neither the evening star nor the morning star, nor any other star ever seen by the eyes of a mortal. It was a new star with a strange and wonderful brilliance, and while we stood there watching it, we saw the star move. It moved slowly and solemnly and continued to come closer to us; and then it stood still. High in the sky it hovered, sending its long, slanted rays to earth. To our astonishment the rays of the star pointed to the stable next to Cornelius's inn there beneath us in Bethlehem. We were filled with wonder when a path of brilliant, silvery light suddenly appeared from there, illuminating the fields and the hills with a glow that almost blinded us. And in that light, more brilliant than the light of the most brilliant sun, we could see the herds with their heads aloft and their eyes directed at the heavens. It was a wonderful sight to see the cattle, sheep and goats, which always stood with their heads turned to the ground, staring up at the heavens – just like us.

"We were too terrified to say a word. We had never seen or heard anything like that before. It felt as if I were dreaming.

"'Did you see it move?' I asked. 'Yes,' said Ephraim. 'Yes,' said Daniel.

"'Look!' said Daniel again and pointed in the direction of the sheep with his shepherd's crook, because he also saw how they stared at the star. It was very quiet. I was filled with fear.

"'What do you think of this, Ephraim?' I whispered with a trembling voice. 'What does this foretell?'

"'No,' he said, 'I don't know the meaning of such things. Perhaps it is the beginning of the end, when God will destroy mankind in His wrath. Oh, woe is me, for my sins are many!'

"Then I looked at Daniel. His face was like that of a dead man, while he mumbled, 'And it will come to pass in the last days, says the Lord, that I will pour my Spirit out upon all flesh. And there will be miracles in the heavens and on the earth.'

"'Yes, look!' he exclaimed suddenly and sprang to his feet. 'Look! It is the end.'

"And from the path of light a radiant figure of the greatest splendour appeared. We fell to our knees, because we were paralysed with fear."

Isaac was silent. Hermas sighed in wonder and astonishment,

and I saw how he looked at the shepherd while he stroked the lamb like someone in a trance.

"And look!" Isaac continued. "The angel spoke to us and said, 'Do not be afraid. I bring you good news of great joy that will be for all the people. Today in the town of David, a Saviour has been born to you; he is Christ the Lord. This will be a sign to you: you will find a baby wrapped in cloths and lying in a manger.'

"While he was speaking, he put out his hand to bless us, and in this manner he ascended to heaven. And while we kept our eyes glued to him, a great company of the heavenly host was with him, so that the sky was illuminated and filled with the flapping of innumerable wings. We could see the glistening of the white wings beneath the stars against the dark blue sky. Some of them were as close to us as that wild fig tree, and throughout the night we heard the lovely sounds of heavenly music, as the choir of angels sang to us. And these were the words of their song: 'Glory to God in the highest, and on earth peace to men on whom His favour rests.'

"Ah, Rebecca! You had not even been born when I heard that song, but it is still resounding in my ears. And when the day is long and the night tedious, and when I cannot sleep, then I hear it once again and it delights me; because it alleviates the tiring task and brings peace and joy on the arduous way. And I know that I will soon hear the angels sing forever.

"While we were still standing there, watching and listening, everything was suddenly quiet and the angels disappeared. But the star still shone brilliantly above the stable. An awesome silence came over us, and for some time we could not say a word.

"Then Ephraim said, 'Come!' and I could see that he was struggling to speak and that he was trembling like a reed in the wind. 'Get up, let us go to Bethlehem to see what has happened there.'

"We rose and went to Bethlehem, as the angel had commanded us to do. 'But what about the sheep, Ephraim?' I asked, because there was some kind of wild beast in the wood on the opposite side. We had heard it before nightfall. But he did not even look back and walked so quickly that one would never say that he was a man of seventy.

"'Don't you think that he who told us to go to see the one Moses and the prophets spoke of, will tend the sheep? Come! Let us go and find the Christ.' Although he had previously always been very devoted in the tending of the sheep, he now walked on, in an even greater hurry, as if nothing else in the world concerned him more than this one matter.

"'But where are you going?' Daniel asked. 'Where in Bethlehem will you find the child?'

"'There!' he answered, as he first pointed at the star and then at Cornelius's stable with his shepherd's crook. We approached the place hastily, trembling as we went. At the entrance we encountered Joseph of Nazareth. Ephraim knew him well, because he too had lived in the city of David some time earlier. But when we reached the place, we did not quite know what to say. Joseph gestured with his hand that we should approach quietly.

"'Hush!' he whispered. 'She is sleeping. She told me to wait here for you. Listen!' And we could hear the cries of a newborn baby. Expectantly Joseph fixed his gaze on the door and when it opened, Rebecca, we saw your mother, Joanna, standing there. She invited us in, and when we were inside we knelt in front of the child with bowed heads – yes, the Christ-child.

"At first we could hardly see him, because there was only one lamp, and we were careful not to hold it too close, for fear of damaging the baby's eyes. But Joseph screened the light from the baby's eyes, and we saw, and kneeled, and worshipped.

"Not that the Christ looked any different from other children in any definable way. He was wrapped in cloths, as the shimmering person had said, and he lay on the straw in the rough manger. But there was something about his appearance that could not be compared to anything we had ever seen before, so that we were compelled to bow our heads.

"Well, Rebecca, since your mother had been present from the beginning, let her tell your friend, the wife of the Roman, the rest of this wonderful story."

Then old Isaac fell silent and stared far into the distance over the hills with a strange and dreamy expression on his face, as if he saw only the child in the manger. He made no attempt to hide the tears in his eyes. Hermas also began to cry, because he had always been very tender of heart. As for me, I was too overcome with emotion to say a word. I saw a tear running down the wrinkled cheek of the shepherd, and I too wanted to weep, although I could not fathom the reason for this.

We sat like that for a long time. Rebecca broke the silence. "Would you take us to that stable, Isaac?" she asked. "I would like to see the place where the child lay once more, and I presume Susanna and Hermas would also like to see it."

"Oh yes, please!" Hermas exclaimed. "Come, Mommy, let us go look at the stable, and at the manger where the Christ-child lay."

"Certainly, my child!" Isaac said. "You will see it. But first, let us eat, because you must be hungry by now". And there on the spot where the brilliant form had appeared so many years before, we ate the food that Isaac had prepared for us with his own hands. Then we left for Bethlehem. It did not take us long to reach the place. It was a rough shelter for livestock, as one normally finds in the hills. Nevertheless, Isaac uncovered his head and bowed low before he stepped inside. With bated breath we followed him, while Hermas's small hand timidly sought mine. It was as if we stood before the Holy of Holies.

"Here are the three partitions still, just as they were then," Isaac said in a muted voice, because to him even the stones of the floor were holy. "The child was born in the middle one, which is a little wider than the others, and he lay in this very manger."

Hermas advanced hesitantly and slowly stroked the hewn rock with his hand. Isaac paid him no heed. He bowed down low. Then he spoke with a voice trembling with love.

"Almost thirty-three years ago, one by the name of Jesus of Nazareth was born to a pure virgin in this stable – the Christ of God. And see, he now lives in Galilee and performs wonderful deeds of love and mercy.

"On this very spot I kneeled down with Ephraim and Daniel that night when the angels sang. There, Joseph the carpenter stood with the lamp in his hand, and here she lay, the one God had chosen to be the mother of the Most High." Once again he kneeled by the manger.

Hermas, who had stood listening to Isaac's words in wonder, now pulled me by the hand and gestured that he wanted to tell me something. "Mommy," he whispered in my ear, as he peered timidly at the manger, "Oh Mommy, can't I lie down in it as the child did?"

I took him in my arms and put him down on the straw. He closed his eyes and smiled, his dark curls falling over the edge of the manger. Never had he been as lovely to me as he was then. If only Scipio were here, I thought. I wished that he could have heard Isaac's tale and seen his son lying in the place that was so holy to the old shepherd.

Suddenly Isaac spoke again. "There is one more thing to tell. We poor shepherds were not the only ones worshipping the child; there were rich and wise people too. A few days after the birth of the child, wise men – magi – arrived here from the East. A star had lighted their way to him – perhaps even the same star that we had seen on the night of his birth.

"They lodged in the house of Cornelius, the Greedy, for a few days, because they had many possessions with them, and a herd of camels. Yet, it is also told that this very Cornelius (whom I know very well), shut his doors to the mother of the child, even though she was exhausted and pregnant. Joseph was but a poor man. And so the magi stayed in the inn where there had been no room for the one they had come to worship. They took great treasures from their bags, and put valuable gifts and a great deal of gold at his feet.

"But now," Isaac continued as he looked in the direction of the inn (because we had left the stable again), "now they say that he does not value gold, nor any other earthly treasure, because he says that it is easier for a camel to pass through the eye of a needle than for a rich man to enter the kingdom of God. He teaches that one should not gather treasures on this earth, but in heaven where nothing can spoil. No, what is more, he is even poorer than the poorest of people. He does not have any money, and the only food he eats is what he receives from the poor.

"'Foxes have holes,' he says, 'and the birds of the air have nests, but the Son of Man (for so he calls himself) has no place to lay his head.' Daniel himself has seen how he sleeps in the open field. And now I would like to tell you women something, but keep it to yourselves. I worked hard for fifty-seven years. I did not squander my money, and never took a wife. What I own, I have hidden in the sheep-pen, and soon I will stop tending sheep and go in search of Jesus. People call me Isaac, the Covetous, but they do not know me. Every penny that I have saved, is for him whom I worshipped – the baby in that stable.

"I will leave everything and follow him. He will never want for food and clothes. He will never have to sleep under the open sky again. He will no longer know what it is to brave hunger or cold or poverty. I have looked for him and longed for him for many years. The time has come.

"I have not seen him for many years, except in my dreams. I heard nothing about him, but in my heart I knew that he would rise one day and lead Israel. And now the entire Galilee has gone to meet him. And I, too, will once again go to him and fall down at his feet ... and worship him. He will not refuse me, because he is gentle and humble of heart. I will follow him wherever he goes. During the day I will listen to his wonderful words, and at night I will guard him and care for him and make sure that nothing does him harm. I will prepare his food, and I will wash his feet when he is tired. I, Isaac the shepherd, long only to be with him, and to go wherever he goes, yes, until the very end. And I will pray that we will not even be separated by death!"

Little could I know, as I listened to him then, how these words would be fulfilled. The angels had sung to him; for years he had lived alone in the hills. What kind of communion he had with the Unseen, no one knows. There was something in his eyes that I had never before seen in any other eyes. Perhaps he could see the things that were still to happen.

"Look!" he said, "the sun is already setting behind the hills; I must return to my sheep." Then he looked at me and said, "Wife of a Roman soldier, if this Nazarene passes within your reach, make sure that you take your son to him to be blessed, because he loves little children and says that the kingdom of heaven belongs to them. Truly, I tell you, the child whose birthplace you saw today, this child born of a virgin, is none other than the Christ – the Son of the Most High. And what I tell you here, is what the angels told me."

When we took our leave, he called Hermas to him. "My boy," he said, "will you also follow the Christ?"

"Yes!" the boy replied with conviction. "I will find him, and I will take the sword and the helmet that Rufus made for me, and I will go out and defeat his enemies."

"Good, my boy! There will be room for such as yourself, because there are many people who do not love him." And he laid his hands on the boy's head, blessed him, and then left.

Night overtook us before we reached Rebecca's house. She was exhausted because of the heat and the day's exertion, and, after all, her time was very near. The following morning at daybreak, her child was born.

Chapter 7

"For unto us a child is born"

In the days that followed, Rebecca and the child gained strength; but I stayed with them. One evening, towards sunset, we sat on the roof and once again talked about the Nazarene. Rebecca asked me to read her something from the prophet Isaiah, while the light still allowed it. I read until I reached the words: "For unto us a child is born, to us a son is given, and the government will be on his shoulders. And he will be called Wonderful Counsellor, Mighty God, Everlasting Father, Prince of Peace."

"Oh, Susanna," she said, "Susanna, friend of my heart, I wish you could see him too! I know that you have prayed for years that he would come, and now he is truly among us. May God prevent that you would be one of those who do not know him!"

"But Rebecca," I said, "could this Jesus truly be God's chosen one? Because I hear that those in power do not acknowledge him, but that they talk of him as one who deceives the people with false teachings. Could this be the mighty one Isaiah spoke about?"

Rebecca did not answer. A great longing filled me and I could not rest. I got up and went to her. With my hands on her shoulders, I spoke to her again. "Rebecca, I beg you, do not deceive me. Do you truly believe, and do you know in your heart, that this Jesus of Nazareth is he, the Christ of God, of whom Moses and the prophets spoke?"

Rebecca got to her feet and clasped her child to her breast. Then she said, "As truly as this child was born from my body, and is flesh of my flesh, bone of my bone, blood of my blood, so truly the child born in the stable is the Christ of God; and that very child, now a man, is he who is now in Galilee, the one the people call Jesus of Nazareth." And suddenly she collapsed onto the bench, exhausted, and gestured for me to approach. "Tomorrow," she continued, "you must go to the house of my mother, Joanna, and she will tell you more about this man. But for now, please help me to my feet, because I am very tired." And we went into the house.

The following morning I went to visit Joanna, who lived close to the southern gate. I had not seen Joanna for many years, and also did not know her very well. Now the years were pressing heavily upon her, although her eyes were still surprisingly bright. She sat beneath a fig tree with her hands folded in her lap, and she was so quiet that I thought she was asleep. When my shadow fell across her face, she looked up and asked, "Woman, who are you?" Her voice was soft and calm, as if it came from far away. "Who are you, and who are you looking for?"

"I am Susanna, the wife of Scipio, the Roman, and I come from your daughter, Rebecca. She sends her regards and love, as well as these olives and this bag of wine, which she has made for you herself."

"Peace be with you, Susanna of Jerusalem!" She hit an amphora with her walking stick and ordered the slave that appeared to fetch water to wash my feet, and to offer me figs and bread and wine.

"Are Rebecca and the child well?" she asked. Then we talked about the two of them for some time. After eating, I poured out my heart to her and spoke about the things concerning Jesus that Rebecca had heard, and how I could not quite decide whether to believe them. I also shared my fears about my husband, Scipio, with her. For a few moments she sat in silence, with her calm eyes, as gentle and full of empathy as those of a dove, fixed upon me. And every morsel of fear left me, and I had only one desire, namely to listen as she spoke about the one she loved.

"Susanna, my daughter," she finally said, "listen to me. I am old and my time is almost up. The tongues of those approaching the grave are guided by the truth, and I fear the Lord. I will never deceive you, my child. I have seen many things in my life. Great is the number of children I have helped bring into this world. I have closed many eyelids, and embalmed many corpses. Soon I, yes, I also, will depart from this world. Therefore I will speak.

"I will now tell you things I have never told anyone else, apart from my daughter, Rebecca and Isaac the shepherd. Perhaps it is for the best that someone else knows; and my heart is filled with a wonderful feeling when I look at you and when I hear you talk about him. So, listen carefully.

"It was late, towards evening, and I sat there where you are sitting now when a man arrived at the house in great distress and asked to see me. He was of middle-age and his hair and beard had already started turning grey. He wore a brown robe made from rough wool, with a girdle tied around his waist. He carried a thick walking stick and seemed to have travelled far, and he was in a great hurry.

"'Peace be with you!' he greeted me. 'Are you the Joanna who previously lived in Nazareth and who knows the art of taking care of women?'

"'Yes, it is as you said,' I replied. 'I am Joanna, and if my eyes are not playing tricks on me, you are Joseph, the carpenter.'

"'Yes, that's correct, and I am in dire need of your expert services.'

"Then he told me how he had come to Bethlehem with his young wife, Mary, and how the inn was so full that they had no choice but to find shelter in the stable. They had travelled south through Galilee from their home in Nazareth, and had been on the road for approximately five days.

"In those days I was still lively and strong. I rose immediately, because Joseph had told me that Mary was about to give birth. I told him to return to her without delay, while I hastily collected clean linen, a water jug, food, and a few other things that I would need, and followed him. I had to make my way through a throng of people, because Bethlehem was particularly full of activity that night, since it was the time of the census. There were crowds of rowdy men and women. Caravans, horses, donkeys and camels were tethered everywhere along the way, while their exhausted drivers were asleep on the ground.

"The place where the child would be born, the place to which I followed Joseph, was a cave in the courtyard of the tribal chief. The cave was partly hewn from the solid rock, and partly constructed from rough stone walls. It bordered on the pastures, from where the cattle could enter it via a narrow passage covered with a slanting thatched roof. A wide wooden door formed the entrance to the cave. That was the stable. You say that you have seen it? It hasn't changed much since the first day I saw it. It did not have a window: the only light came in through the door. The floor was paved with stone, and was covered by a thick layer of straw. There was plenty of hay and bedding for the cattle.

"In that humble place I met Mary, God's blessed one, for the first time, and even if I were to live twice as long as is destined for a person, her face will always seem fresh and lovely to me. She rose and welcomed me with a smile. 'Peace be with you!' she said. 'I thank you with all my heart for coming to my aid in my time of need.' And again she smiled at me, so that I could not stop myself from loving her. My soul went out to her, and I knew that I would love her until my eyes were one day finally closed in the sleep of death.

"Susanna, I wish I could find the words to tell you about that incomparable virgin. I can describe her countenance, but what I read in her eyes cannot be put into words. She was as beautiful as the flowers of the field, and pure as the morning dew. I know I will never witness a more beautiful face until I leave this earth and witness the faces of the children of God. That humble stable was hallowed ground, hallowed by her presence. Her dress was made from a soft white fabric, although it was dusty from the journey. It shone as if she was far removed from earthly things, and although she was in a stable, she did not belong to it. Her presence made the place of her confinement a holy place.

"After I had recovered (because I had forgotten myself entirely) I gathered some of the straw lying about, and with the cloaks and the cloth of the donkey I made her a bed, because she was very tired. With a sigh she lay down and smiled weakly at me, with weary eyes. I remember well how those very eyes, which contrasted clearly with the pale face, followed me as I went about my business. I gave her the bread and olives and dried figs I had brought along, while Joseph heated the goat's milk on the fire in the front cave. When everything was ready, she asked me to join her, and with bowed heads and folded hands she thanked God. Then we all enjoyed our meal together.

"Later I rose and prepared a more comfortable bed for her, but Mary preferred to stand about and to move, which was wise. Every now and again an intense pain shot through her body, and her eyes filled with tears. Yet she did not complain once, but spoke to me in a friendly way and thanked me for everything I did, even if I simply wiped her brow.

"A little girl arrived from the inn with a bunch of flowers and asked whether there was anything she could do. I still remember the expression of awe and respect in her eyes when she saw Mary's face. Her tears were close to the surface when I told her that we had everything we needed and that she could leave.

"Mary took the flowers and wove a wreath, and then placed it in the manger I had prepared for the baby, and then turned aside to dry her tears. My heart was filled with an overwhelming sense of longing and empathy, as I had never before felt for any woman I had tended. There was something inexplicable about this gentle and humble virgin from Nazareth that I have never seen in any other. As she was standing there with bowed head, her one hand caressing the manger, the other covering her face, while she cried quietly, I thought my heart would break. I went to her and placed my hand on her shoulder, because she was shaking. 'No, my child,' I said, 'don't be afraid. Be strong, because the time of your delivery is near.'

"She looked at me with such a lovely smile that my love towards her intensified even more. Pure and holy her eyes shone through her tears. 'Please forgive me,' she said, 'perhaps you misunderstand. It's not the pain,' (her hand went to her side and her lips trembled from the grief she had to endure) 'no,' and once again she smiled, 'it's not the pain. But I wonder, and I fear – everything is so wonderful to me,' and in her eyes I saw a light I could not understand.

"'Have you heard the prophecy that a child will be born from a virgin?' she asked.

"'Yes, of course!' I replied, and then she seemed to relax a little. 'Listen to me, Joanna,' she whispered. 'In evil days people will suspect me. Perhaps you have heard, Joanna, that it was in Nazareth, in the cool of the day, that the angel appeared to me. I was sitting under the palm trees, enjoying the lovely fragrance of the flowers I had picked, when a soft voice, like the rustling of the leaves, called my name and told me that wonderful things would happen to me.

"'In a short while I will have to endure the pain of labour. To some it is the valley of death. If it were to be my fate to enter that valley, I want you to know that an angel truly did appear to me and told me that I would give birth to a boy; and that the child that would be born from me, would be the Son of God, and that his name would be Jesus.

"'Joanna, I have not been with any earthly man. I am the wife of Joseph, but he has never been with me as a husband.'

"Exhausted she collapsed on the rough bed and hid her face in her hands. I kneeled by her side and touched her gently. 'Mary,' I said, 'servant of the Most High, I know that you are telling the truth. I have heard much about this very matter in the synagogue since my youth.'

"She lay there, ashen in colour, as if chiselled from the whitest marble, and as I saw her lying there, a great fear filled me at the thought of what lay in store for her, because she appeared so weak and fragile. I softly walked to the other cave and told Joseph to prepare hot water. The night was quiet and clear, and the sky was strewn with stars. The lights of the inn were out; Bethlehem slept.

In the distance, on the hills, a sheep bleated; then everything was silent.

"I thought about everything this woman had told me. How wonderful that the One who lives beyond the stars and guarded Bethlehem, chose this humble one to be the mother of His child – and I, yes, I was there to witness it. It was all too wonderful for me to comprehend. For a moment I breathed in the night air, and then I returned to the inner stable.

"It was as if my soul had been anointed and my heart cleansed. Everything was as I had left it: the lamp still flickered in the corner, the donkey and the oxen ate their fodder while they slowly surveyed their surroundings, the straw lay on the ground in a heap. At the manger the basin with milk and the jug of water stood, and, yes, she whom I came to care for was also there.

"Yes, everything was still the same, and yet not the same, because the rough cave was the Holy of Holies to me, the smoking wick was the holy fire; the pleasant breath of the oxen was the holy incense; and that manger was the altar of God, where heaven and earth would meet.

"Even more: she with the pale, worn face and the dark, sad eyes, she with the frail, suffering body and the dripping tears, was the servant of the Most High who had to bring the only begotten Son of God into this human world. I kneeled, bowed my head, and prayed.

"She rose and took out the baby clothes. She pressed them to her cheek, perhaps to feel whether they were dry, and then placed them in the manger while she smiled at me through her tears. Then she leaned against the manger and folded her arms across her breast. She lifted her eyes to the heavens and began speaking softly.

"'Don't be afraid, Mary, because you have found God's grace. The Holy Spirit will fill you and the power of the Most High will envelop you. Therefore the Holy One that will be born will also be called the Son of God. Yes Lord,' and her hands grasped her breasts, and her voice rose in sorrowful supplication. 'Yes, Lord, the actual Son of God!'

"A shudder of tormenting pain shook that weak body. She fell to her knees and grasped the sides of the manger with her hands. She was extremely short of breath, and her heart was beating rapidly. Tears ran down her tortured, pale face like droplets of rain and mixed with her cold sweat. Again she lifted her face to heaven and prayed through her half-smothered sobs.

"'I thank You, my Father in heaven, that You chose my body to be broken, my blood to be spilled, for You. Give me strength to drink this cup. Let Your promise be fulfilled now – let the power of the Most High envelop me. Yes, Lord, let it be fulfilled.'

"Then she got up like one filled with new strength, and stretched out her arms as if she could see things I could not. The lamplight illuminated her face, her pale lips moved, but I heard no sound.

"I wanted to go to her, but she kept me away with an outstretched hand.

"'No, Joanna,' she said, 'wouldn't you please first kneel down and pray for the child that has to be born?'

"As befits mortals in the presence of those who are holy, I knelt and bowed my head and tried to pray, but I hardly knew what to say. I felt rested and calm as if in the very presence of God. I heard the deep breathing of the oxen and the crackling of the fire outside. I closed my eyes and prayed that the fragile, beautiful body of the mother would be spared.

"In that holy atmosphere, nothing broke the silence; no ox stirred in its stable. Once again Mary kneeled down, and her face was radiant with the sheen of the glorious beings that had descended from heaven to sanctify the birthplace of the Redeemer of Israel. Oh, Susanna, the heavenly music, lovely and soft and gentle, that broke over my soul in waves! Perhaps it was the rustling of the wings of the angels, because it appeared as though all of heaven was there to await the coming of the King.

"Never before, as far as I can remember, had I fallen asleep when I had to sit up at the childbed of a woman. I do not know whether it perhaps was because of the heat of the lamp or of the cattle, or because of something else, but I fell into a deep sleep. Although I am an old woman now, I have always reproached myself for this. What would Mary have thought if she had to know that

I did not keep vigil during her labour?

"And yet, perhaps that sleep was ordained by God himself, so that no human eyes, except for those of his chosen servant, would witness the coming of His only begotten Son to this sinful world. I do not know how long I slept. I was woken by a soft weeping (I have always been a very light sleeper): it was the sorrowful weeping of a little baby. For behold, while I was asleep, Mary's child had been born. And so it came to pass that Christ was born in Bethlehem.

"The joy in the heart of that mother when she saw her son for the first time can only be described by the angels, because no mortal tongue could ever tell that wonderful tale.

"Wide awake, I asked to be forgiven for neglecting my duty, and immediately I made haste to tend to the mother and child. Ah, Susanna! Will I ever forget that expression of holy joy in those dark, tearful eyes as the woman looked at the child she had given birth to? She did not hear my words of self-reproach, because her heart was filled with joy.

"Slowly the child opened his eyes and looked unblinkingly at his mother. Slowly the small head turned, and the child looked at the oxen; and then he turned his gaze to me, and my heart was filled with love and compassion. And that is how I see him to this day. We wrapped the child in cloths and placed him in the manger. His mother bowed down over him and kissed him.

"Suddenly we were enveloped by an incredibly brilliant light. Lovely musical tones, as had never before been heard by any mortal, sounded in our ears. The oxen stirred restlessly in their stable; the donkey got up and listened. I was overcome by a great fear.

"'Mary, mother of the child the prophets have called wonderful; you who spoke with angels in this night, tell me where this wonderful light is coming from, and this heavenly music in the middle of the night.'

"'No, listen, Joanna,' she said, 'can't you hear the voice that is speaking so softly and clearly? Listen to the words he is speaking.'

"My heart sank, because she was weak, very weak, and I was afraid that she was delirious.

"'Blessed one,' I said, 'you must rest. Rest a while.' But she stood there in a tense posture with the baby pressed to her breast.

"'Listen! Can't you hear it? The voice that speaks like the song of birds: "Today in the town of David a Saviour has been born to you; He is Christ the Lord."'

"I listened, but the music had stopped and all was quiet. The only sounds I could hear were the crackling fire and the breathing of the oxen, as well as the pounding of my own heart – yes, and hers too. With a cry of distress I went to her, but she paid me no heed.

"Of course I know now that she was not delirious, because that was what the brilliant being told the shepherds. But no one can explain how she had heard the same words almost six miles from that place. And then suddenly the night was filled with powerful singing – yes, and in the stable too, as if the brilliant beings floated above the child. My ears were no longer shut and I could hear the words they sang: 'Glory to God in the highest, and on earth peace to men on whom His favour rests.' Then the singing died away and the great light grew dimmer and disappeared, and the lamp cast strange shadows everywhere.

"I got up," Joanna continued, "and prepared food for Mary. I encountered Joseph where he was waiting in fear and trembling. He immediately enquired about the child, because he had heard the crying, and then he went to them. When I returned to the inner stable, I found him kneeling with bowed head at the manger. He got up and asked whether there was anything he could do. I told him to go out to heat up more water, because at times like these men are, more often than not, in the way.

"With a strength that surprised me, the young mother sat up straight, took the food, and said grace. And when she ate, the child made a joyful sound. His eyes were wide open and a smile played over his lips; and everything that is, was or will ever be heavenly, was embodied in that smile.

"Wistfully the mother looked at her child, and while she was looking at him she was overcome by anxiety, for she whispered the words of Isaiah: 'He was despised and rejected by men, a man of sorrows, and familiar with suffering,' (she whispered almost inaudibly), '– he was led like a lamb to the slaughter – yet he took up our infirmities and carried our sorrows.'

"'O Isaiah,' she called out, 'prophet of the Most High, did you truly prophesy these things about my son?'

"Silent tears filled her eyes and fell on the face of Jesus as the mother whispered the words, 'Man of sorrows'. Gently she wiped the tears from the face of her child, and then it seemed as if an even greater anxiety took a hold of her, because with an even louder voice she called out, 'Isaiah, did you foresee my broken body and spilled blood, when you predicted the broken body and spilled blood of my son? Oh, my son! My son!' and a cold sweat appeared on her brow.

"Then a wonderful calm descended upon her. Perhaps an angel, or Isaiah himself whispered to her, 'Leave the things that must come to him in the hands of Him who holds the fate of worlds and of people. And when he tears the veil that covers the eyes, may your eyes see how your son sacrifices himself of his own free will for the salvation of the world.'

"But I know nothing of these things. What the overwhelmed mother saw or heard was hidden from me, but she lifted her eyes to heaven and wiped her tears. She asked me to lay the child beside her and then whispered with a smile of wonderful resignation, 'Your will be done.'

"Then she took the child against her breast and lulled him to sleep with a melody from her childhood while his tiny fingers gripped her silky hair. The melody grew softer until it died away altogether, and when I looked again, both mother and child were fast asleep.

"I went out to Joseph and told him not to allow anyone to enter. And when I looked at him I saw that he was as pale as her whom I had just left.

"'How are the mother and the child?' he immediately wanted to know. 'Well,' I replied. 'They are sleeping. Stay calm. Do not be troubled, everything will be fine.'

"'No, but I am afraid for the child. Joanna, I do not know what to say, because I have seen wonderful signs and things in the air. Tonight my eyes were opened. God granted me a vision. A star with a blinding brilliance, like no other star in the heavens, appeared and revealed all the hills and valleys to me, as if they were lying in the sun at noon, except that the light was white. And behold, on that hill you see before you, a big cross appeared – the cross-beam stretched from east to west, from sunrise to sunset. And while I was staring at it, the star hovered above the cross, a lonely and sombre cross. It appeared to me that its shadow covered the entire world, and in its shadow I saw a tomb – a tomb of death. And I was filled with fear.'

"'But as I was looking, a cloud obstructed the cross, and for a moment everything was covered in darkness. Then a light appeared that grew in brilliance. And the tomb – I could see – was broken open and empty, and the light shone from within the tomb. Then the cross itself began to emit light, and the shadow became a path of light, and the entire world was filled by the glow of heaven, so that I had no choice but to shut my eyes and cover my face. When I looked again, nothing could be seen apart from what you can see now.'

"For a moment he said nothing and looked at me in fear. 'But what does it all mean,' I asked.

"'No, woman, I don't know, but I am afraid for the child. Please go and see whether Mary doesn't want for something. And please keep all of this to yourself. Peace be with you!'

"I left him immediately and went inside. I was busy fixing the wick of the lamp when I heard the sound of footsteps. I went to open the door, and before me stood shepherds from the fields of Bethlehem. With great joy they told me about the heavenly host who sang to them, and how they had left their sheep on the instruction of the angel and had come to worship the child.

"'We were told that we would find him in a manger and wrapped in cloths,' one of them, called Ephraim, said.

"Only after Mary had rested well, did I allow the shepherds inside. At the manger they kneeled down and worshipped, while Ephraim said, 'Just as the angel told us.' And after they had laid their gifts at the feet of Jesus, they left, praising and glorifying God. So it came to pass that these simple people from the field were among the first mortals to worship Christ.

"O Susanna, my daughter, can you doubt that he is truly the Christ? No! I know you believe this in your heart. Listen to me. One of these days I will go to Jerusalem to see him once again, because he is travelling there. My days are numbered, but I will see him, and kneel and worship him – the one I tended in that stable. It was given to me to know that I will not close my eyes in the sleep of death before all these things have come to pass."

Joanna's wonderful tale had come to an end. The sun was already high in the sky, and she was exhausted from all the talking. She asked me to lead her to her bench, and then she blessed me and asked me to warn the Nazarene against danger if I were to encounter him upon my return to Jerusalem.

With mixed feelings of joy and sadness I departed and returned to the house of Rebecca.

Chapter 8

Prophet of Love

Two days later I returned to Jerusalem with my son Hermas. Rebecca, who accompanied us for a short distance, spoke a lot about the Messiah along the way. I was very sad because I had to say goodbye to someone I had learned to love, and from whom I had heard about a love greater than that of this earth. There in the young grass of the field, our way lighted by the glory of the sun, and the air filled with the fragrance of flowers, we embraced and said our goodbyes. Rebecca whispered a name into my ear, the name that was holy to me now; perhaps the same name Isaac, the shepherd, had whispered into the ear of Hermas.

We had only walked a short distance when Hermas said cheerfully, "Mommy, I like the Nazarene Isaac spoke of, a lot. Will you take me to see him one day? I heard everything the shepherd said about the angels and the camels that came across the desert, about the wonderful star and the oxen in the stable. Mommy, will you take me to the Nazarene, because I will surely love him. I love him already, even though I have never seen him."

Wonderful words for such a young child, I thought. What spirit works inside us that a child, without having seen him, already loves him? My eyes had not looked upon him either, and yet I knew that my soul longed for him.

It was late when we arrived in Jerusalem, because I had first tended the wounds of someone who was injured, in the house of Ben Ezra. The gate was already shut, and when the gatekeeper in the watch tower heard my calls, he asked, "Who is it that disturbs the peace at such a late hour?"

"I am Susanna, the wife of Scipio, and even though it is very late, I would be very grateful if you would let me in."

"Yes, fine, woman, you are always welcome in this disordered city," he said, half-asleep, and then he opened the small gate for us. "Your husband will receive you with joy, because only yesterday morning he told me that you would be returning shortly. Have you heard anything about the Galilean prophet? There are many rumours about him in the city."

When Hermas heard this he wanted to tell the guard everything he had heard, but we had to hurry home. In spite of the late hour, Scipio and Nidia welcomed us joyfully, and for the first time in many days we sat down together at the table to eat something. I was exhausted from the journey and also overwhelmed with joy to be with my loved ones again, with the result that I spoke very little. But Hermas wanted to tell everything and could talk of nothing but Isaac, the shepherd, and the manger of the child Jesus, and how he would one day become a soldier and fight for him. Scipio said nothing, but I could see that he did not approve. Nidia, on the other hand, questioned the boy carefully about the birth of the child and about everything old Isaac had said.

"You have made a mistake, Susanna," Scipio said when the children had gone to bed. "This Isaac has filled the boy's head with ideas. He can talk of nothing else than sheep and oxen and mangers and shepherds and such. I wish he would not think about this Nazarene. The man you call Jesus is an enemy of Rome and must inevitably come to a fall."

"No, Scipio," I replied (and I was surprised at my own boldness). "He is truly the Christ of God and will lead Israel to glory."

"Woman, you are out of your mind! The heat of the sun must have affected your head. You don't know what you are saying."

"Oh, Scipio, listen to me. I beg you, please don't fight against him, because it will be in vain. He cannot be defeated. He is already on his way to Jerusalem to make the might of Rome the footstool of Israel, just as the prophets have said."

"Ha, ha, ha!" Scipio laughed. "Israel itself will make a footstool of him. Listen to me, woman! Only yesterday I spoke to one of the temple guards. 'Scipio,' he said, 'if the Nazarene comes to Jerusalem, then he will meet his end. Caiaphas and those who side with him are waiting for him. The men of the Sanhedrin are like hungry wolves who have caught wind of their prey, because they are determined to kill this Galilean.' No, woman," he continued, "do not be depressed. You are tired and upset. It is best that you go to bed."

I was exhausted and extremely disappointed that he had reacted so violently against the Nazarene. However, I very much wanted to discuss the things that I had heard from Rebecca with him. Perhaps if he knew what really happened, he would believe. But my heart was heavy within me.

"Scipio," I said, "I want you to know that I have loved you always, and that I have been faithful as a wife and as a mother. I wish that we could be one absolutely in heart and in faith. I cannot hide anything from you. I cannot and shall not deceive you. You have listened to me in the past – I know your heart is not as hard as your words. I know you dislike the Jews and would rather live among your own people, because you have not found rest in this strange country.

"You know nothing about Judaism, because the arrogance of the priests has prejudiced your mind. But I want you to know that their interpretation of the law of Moses does not correspond with that of the Nazarene. His teachings are of a great redeeming love. I fear that you are angry with me, but I want to tell you everything that I have heard and seen concerning the Nazarene. If only you are willing to listen to me, I will gladly share the good news with you."

"Enough!" he shouted, his anger growing. "You have already poisoned the minds of Nidia and Hermas with your talk of this Galilean. Have you forgotten that the priests regard him as a swindler who does nothing but perform magic tricks? Most people around here agree that nothing good has ever come from Nazareth, and yet you want to cling to this false prophet, the son of a carpenter, who will be hauled before the Sanhedrin one of these days for treason. Even as we speak, as I have told you before, they are lying in wait for him."

"Oh, Scipio," I said, "please don't talk like that about someone who speaks only of forgiveness; someone who loves all people and only longs that they should love each other."

"Susanna," Scipio said, furiously, "I am a soldier in the legion of the army of Tiberius, and a freeborn citizen of Rome. I have been taught to be faithful to Caesar. He says that a sharp sword is a man's faithful friend, and now you speak of someone who wants me to love my enemy!"

"Scipio, oh, please do not allow something to come between us! Please have a little patience with me. Have you forgotten the days and nights when you lay seriously injured in the mountains of Gadara? What would have become of you if I had regarded you as nothing but an enemy of Israel? Yet, although I discovered someone of a strange race, perhaps fatally wounded, I tended your wounds and looked after you until you had regained your health and were fit to walk again. And when you married me, you promised that, even though we were not of the same faith, you would always allow me to serve the God of Israel. And when I whispered in your ear, 'Scipio, what if we were to have children?' you answered, 'Susanna, the children that will be born to us will choose between my gods and the God that you serve.'

"Scipio, I feel that great things are about to happen. I have been filled with a grief that I cannot put into words. Here on my scroll I have written down many of the sayings of Jesus, as I heard them from Joanna, the mother of Rebecca. Listen to these words, Scipio, that he spoke in Galilee: 'I am going to prepare a place for you, that you also may be where I am.' Oh, Scipio, it bores you to listen to me now, but have you considered that the day may come when you will no longer hear my voice, nor I yours? For us, as for all people, the great silence approaches. Can you believe that death signals the end of all things? My heart would break if I did not, by faith, see eternal life waiting for us somewhere on the other side of the grave. On my scroll is written: 'He who believes in Me, has eternal life.' What would this eternal life mean to me, Scipio, if you did not find it also, or Nidia, or Hermas? Would you rather see that we die like the dogs in the marketplace and be thrown onto the fires of Gehenna?

"This prophet speaks of a kingdom of God, a kingdom that may already be established here, now, a kingdom of peace and love, a kingdom for all who follow his will. And yet, because he proclaims that we should love our fellow human beings, he must suffer at the hands of the unbelievers. Scipio, have you ever heard of such a wonderful love?"

"Susanna," he said, and it appeared to me as though his voice was somewhat softer, "I desire no other love than yours. The Galilean has enchanted you. Never mention that name before me again. Forget that you ever heard about this dreamer, because your foolishness may reach the ears of Licinius, or even those of my lord Pilate."

Yet, I could not forget, because when I lay down to rest, I knew that the Nazarene truly was the Son of the Most High. Through my tears I prayed that Scipio would not harden his heart towards him.

(Here ends the writings of Susanna.)

Chapter 9

The Nazarene finds a young champion

On the first day of the week after my wife Susanna had returned from Bethlehem, I was standing on the Mount of Olives when I saw a large crowd of people coming from the direction of Bethany. When they got close, I saw someone among them riding on a donkey while the crowd cheered and sang.

"Hosanna!" they cried. "Blessed is He who comes in the name of the Lord."

While I stood watching, one of the Pharisees came to me and said heatedly that I should arrest the man on the donkey. "He is causing the people to become disloyal," he said, "and he speaks ill of Caesar."

I summoned Probus and a few other soldiers of the garrison and asked them to come with me. When we arrived at the city gate, we could not get close to him because of the pressing crowd. We climbed onto the city wall and waited there. Probus burst out laughing. "Is this the man who wants to shake the throne of Caesar?" he asked. "Look at his war-horse!" he mocked, while pointing at the donkey foal. "Look at his army!" and he nodded towards the children walking in front and waving palm branches in the air. The crowd kept growing as the procession passed through the camps, past the tents of the pilgrims who had come to celebrate the Passover. Some of them also ran out with green branches and took off their cloaks and threw them before the feet of the donkey.

"But who is he?" I asked a priest.

"Who else but Jesus, the blasphemer," Probus answered. "The people are crazy about him."

I very much wanted to see his face, but because of the crowd I could not. But I laughed. Someone like him, surrounded by people such as these, would never pose any threat to the Roman rulers. I had expected to see a king leading an army, and here was a man clothed in white, with a donkey as transport. And his followers hailed him as the king of the Jews. I laughed again.

"Hosanna!" the children called out.

"Hosanna!" the crowd answered.

"Hosanna!" Probus mocked, in a feigned woman's voice. And then a few priests came to Jesus, and the crowd fell silent to hear what they said. I heard the voice of the Galilean when he answered, "I tell you, if they keep quiet, the stones will cry out."

"Ha, ha, ha!" Probus laughed. "Listen, Scipio, he says that the stones will call out. One of these days the Jews will find enough stones to bring an end to his calls, or else he will hang from the tree of death. Back to the dice, Scipio! That pretender will only hurt himself, and, after all, we are too few to arrest him now. Remember, it's my turn."

That afternoon we were busy with our work in the workshop when Hermas arrived, his outer garment covered in blood.

"What happened to you?" I asked. "Did you hurt yourself?"

"No, Daddy, it's nothing," he said.

"Come, my son, tell me everything. Were you in a fight?"

"Yes," he answered as he washed his hands. He seldom fought, although he was agile and strong for his age. Yet I knew that he had enough of his father's blood to turn into a lion if someone angered him.

"Why did you fight?"

"It happened like this, Daddy. I went to stand near the temple of the Jews to see Jesus. There were many people, and I spoke to Samuel, a Jewish boy, and asked him if he had ever seen Jesus.

And then he replied, 'No, but I am standing here waiting for that false prophet, so that I can spit on him if I can get close enough.' Then I got angry and we fought. But suddenly someone grabbed me, and Samuel too, and pulled us apart. Oh, and he had strong hands, Daddy. He grabbed me by the shoulder and Samuel by the belt, and no matter how hard we tried and gnashed our teeth, we could not get to each other. Then I turned to see who was holding me. I wanted to bite his hand because I was very angry, but when I looked in his eyes, the anger left me. He did not look angry, but calm and friendly. He also looked tired. Then I felt so ashamed that I had been angry, and I lowered my head.

"'My children,' he said, 'why are you fighting?'

"'It happened like this,' I said. 'This boy called Jesus a false prophet, and then I called him a dog and a liar, and then we fought.'

"'But do you think,' he asked, 'that this Jesus would like to see you fighting like this?'

"'I don't know,' I replied. 'But I know this: Samuel hit me on my cheek, and then I remembered that my mommy told me that Jesus had said something about turning the other cheek. So I turned my other cheek towards him, and then he hit me again. Then I could not remember any other instruction, so I hit him as hard as I could.'

"A big man, who was standing behind the stranger, burst out laughing, I don't know why. But then the stranger turned and said, as if he were their superior: 'Quiet, Peter!' But I don't think he was very angry with Peter, because when he looked at us again, his eyes weren't so stern.

"Then someone came towards the stranger through the crowd and said, 'Jesus, I beg you, please come and speak a healing word to my son, for he is ill.'

"Then I knew, Daddy, that it was Jesus himself. Many people surrounded us. I was in a lot of pain, because the boy had hit me very hard, but Jesus put his hand on my head, and immediately all the pain was gone. He put his other hand on the head of the Jewish boy, and then he told us, 'My children, I pray that you will always resist all quarrels, and that you will live in peace. For that is why I came to this world: to proclaim love for all people. So much of the suffering in this world is caused by the wicked tempers of people.'

"Then he said something about war and fighting that stains the world with blood. I cannot remember everything he said, Daddy, but he did say, 'Before the end arrives, a brotherhood of all nations and languages will exist around my broken body.'

"Samuel and I embraced and swore an oath of peace. And then I told Jesus that I had been in Bethlehem, in the stable, and that I had lain in the manger in which he was born. He smiled.

"His eyes became sad, and as he left, he said, 'The kingdom of heaven belongs to such as these.' And, Daddy, his voice was so wonderfully gentle, and he spoke in Aramaic, the same language that Mommy speaks to me when we are alone."

"He doesn't know what is good for boys," I told Hermas, although I was not displeased about what had happened. "They say that only people with little sense follow him. I do not think that he is a very brave man."

"No, Daddy," he answered, "He saw us as he was leaving the temple, where he had personally whipped the people who were selling things and changing money. He drove everyone out and hit them. A friend of Samuel, who had stolen two doves, told us all about it."

"Don't speak like that to the child," Rufus said to me. "You can see that he loves him. And let them say what they may about Jesus, no one can call him a coward, because he fears no man." He returned to his work, while Hermas picked up a piece of wood and started cutting it into the shape of a shepherd's crook.

Chapter 10

The hour and the power of darkness

There is always trouble in Jerusalem at Passover. People from all the surrounding regions come to the city in their thousands and camp on the hills outside the city walls. We, who belong to the guard do not like Passover at all. The Jews despise us, but they hate us even more during this period. They are present in such large numbers at this time of year, that they become quite presumptuous, and it is not an easy task to belong to the garrison. Only a few of the soldiers of the garrison were in Jerusalem, and the Jews caused a great deal of trouble. The guards on Antonia were doubled; everyone had to stay in the garrison; and no one got leave of absence. The governor had just returned to the city from Caesarea and had taken up residence in the palace next to the Praetorium, while Herod Antipas resided in his own palace on Mount Zion. Strife and conflict were in the air.

It was the sixth day after Susanna's return from Bethlehem. Licinius came to the workshop and instructed us to make two crosses for two thieves from the gang of Manlius who had been arrested. When I went into the courtyard to order the slaves to bring in some beams, I saw a new slave. He was a short man with sly eyes, and entirely too forward for my liking. His bent nose betrayed him as a son of Israel.

"Where are you from, and who sent you here?" I asked him.

"I am from Macedonia, master," he replied. "Licinius, the centurion, said that I should come here, because Alexander has a fever."

Judging from his speech, I doubted whether he had ever seen Macedonia. I did not like him at all, but could not say anything. However, I kept a close eye on him. I stood watching how he stripped the bark from the log and levelled the wood with axe and adze, before cutting it to a length of approximately eight yards. He knew what he was doing and did it well. It was my custom to take care of this matter, although there were some who did not make use of these supports. I once saw a crucified man fall from the cross because the nails tore through his hands. Caius made the cross-beam and we nailed it in place. Probus and Varus completed the other cross, and then we went to eat our midday meal.

"Look," Varus said, as he got up and took the cross on his shoulders, "here goes old Archipas of the legion. I would gladly make one of these for him," and he stumbled across the courtyard.

"And here goes Maximus with the twisted foot," Caius said, as he took up the other cross and stumbled towards Varus like a drunken man, according to Maximus's custom. For a while they carried on having fun in this manner while Probus and the others roared with laughter. I did not approve. I prefer a battle to a crucifixion. I went to Rufus, because it was our custom to fence with the swords after the midday meal. When I turned, I saw that Varus had put down his cross and was drinking. The new slave took the cross on his shoulders and stumbled towards Varus.

"And here goes that crook, that magician from Nazareth," he said, and then he kneeled as if he wanted to pray. Probus laughed, but while the slave was still kneeling, Hermas jumped at him and hit him in the face, his eyes filled with anger. And I was proud of the boy, because the blow was well placed, so that the jester landed on his back. Quickly he sprang up and made a terrible row.

"You whelp from hell!" he shouted.

Hermas remained standing in front of him, his face red with

indignation, and he wanted to hit the slave again.

"Stand back, you child of Satan!" Probus called, laughing, and caught the child in his strong arms. Then he turned to the slave and said, "So, mighty prophet, let's hear you pray and prophesy for us."

Thereupon Hermas wrested himself free from Probus's grip and hit him in the face with surprising force. Probus turned purple with anger. "You devil!" he shouted at the child and gave him a blow to the head that sent him reeling to the ground.

Like a leopard pouncing on his prey, I sprang onto Probus (for no one had noticed me at the door) and struck him to the ground, where he remained like a wounded bull in the amphitheatre. Before he could rise, my dagger was in my hand, and I would have killed him in anger had an iron grip not restrained me.

"Quiet!" Rufus whispered in my ear. "Here comes Licinius." When I turned, Licinius was standing in the doorway. I do not know whether he had seen us. But by all the gods, I believe that he had, even though he did not say anything.

"Have you finished the job I gave you?" he asked.

"Yes," Rufus said, while he stood in front of me so that I could put away my dagger.

"Well, make another one; it may be necessary." And with those words he left.

As he said this, I happened to be looking at the slave. He had a furtive smile of evil understanding on his face, the likes of which I had never seen before; yet, as I was looking, it disappeared.

They lifted Probus and put him on the bench, and poured wine into his mouth, while I stood to the side with my hands hooked in my belt. I wished that he would never open his eyes again, but as I watched, his eyelids fluttered and a loud groan escaped from his lips.

"Let him be," Rufus said. "He will be all right in a moment." He poured the rest of the wine over Probus's face with the words: "If something is to bring him to his senses, it would be this!"

We resumed our work, more quietly than usual. Suddenly I froze. "Where is that wretched slave?" I asked. He had disappeared; and no one had seen him leave.

That evening I was dismayed when I got home. My anxiety did not diminish when I found that Susanna was not home to welcome me.

"Where is your mother?" I asked Nidia.

"She went to tend to a sick woman near the Sheep Gate."

We ate in silence. Neither the singing of the boy, nor Nidia playing on the lute, which I usually found so calming, could dispel the nasty premonition that took possession of me. I sent the two children off to bed. It grew dark as I was sitting there thinking about all the wonderful things that had taken place. The more I thought, the more anxious my mind grew. Someone who has encountered blood and death as many times as I have, senses impending trouble in his bones. And that is how I felt. I was also very worried about Susanna because many thieves and robbers and other scoundrels come to Jerusalem during the feast. During this time it was more dangerous for a woman to walk the streets alone. I could not sit still but paced up and down, cursing intermittently. It was very late when she arrived, her face as ashen as death.

"Woman, what is the matter?" I asked.

Her lips moved but she made no sound. She touched her throat and smiled amid her exhaustion. Then she stumbled forward, and would have fallen, had I not caught her in time. I carried her to the bench and laid her down. After a while she opened her eyes.

"Oh, Scipio," she sobbed, "they have arrested him!"

"Who did they arrest?" I asked, surprised.

"Jesus! Jesus the Nazarene – the Christ. They have taken him to Caiaphas. They want to kill him."

I fetched her some wine and food and sat down beside her. She was extremely restless and despondent. "Come, tell me everything," I said. And this is what she told me:

"I did not know the woman at the Sheep Gate. The hour of her labour was near, and she was so ill that I had little hope for her. In her delirium she called out many things, but the name of her husband, Nereus, was constantly on her lips.

"'Where is this Nereus?' I asked the servant. 'He has to see her. She will die before daybreak.'

"'He went with a detachment of the guard,' she said.

"'But where?' I asked.

"'No, I do not know.'

"The woman deteriorated. 'She must see him soon,' I thought, 'or it will be too late.' She grew quieter, although the pain was very bad.

"' Nereus! Nereus!' she called.

"'Yes,' I said, 'where is he so that I can bring him to you?'

"'Listen!' she said. "He told me where he was going, but I am not allowed to tell anyone. Nereus! Nereus! My beloved! Where are you?' And for some time she did not know what she was saying. Then she lay exhausted and quiet.

"'Where is he, your Nereus?' I whispered in her ear.

"'He commands a detachment, but not for a fight. They went to arrest one man. No one will wound him. Oh, Caiaphas! Why did you take my Nereus away from me?'

"'But where did the detachment go?'

"'Across the stream to the garden. They are only going to arrest one man. No one would hurt my Nereus. And yet, what keeps you, my husband?'

"'But what is the name of the garden?'

"'Gethsemane – Gethsemane.'

"I was about to send the servant to look for the man, when a cry sounded from the bed. I knew that it was too late. She died a few moments later."

Susanna looked at me and shuddered.

"Well, and what happened then?" I asked.

"Oh, Scipio! The child, the child that was born, was no human being – it was a monster."

"Not a human being!" I said. "That comes as no surprise, because the father himself, this Nereus, is known as a monster among the entire legion. Do you think the womb of a woman could bring forth anything pure from such seed? If the lion were to give birth to a lamb, and the eagle to a dove, a bigger wonder would have occurred than anything the miracle-worker you talk about all day, has ever done."

Susanna covered her eyes with her hand and did not say anything. I comforted her as best I could, and wanted to carry her to her bed, but she did not want to go.

"No, listen, Scipio," she said, "there is more to tell. I left the house and hurried here, while I tried all the time to think of all manner of things to take my mind off what I had seen, when I suddenly could not go on. I had to stop. The woman's cries still sounded in my ears: 'Oh, Caiaphas! Why did you take my Nereus away from me? They are only going to arrest one man there on the other side of the stream. Gethsemane! Gethsemane!' And I understood. They had gone to arrest the Nazarene. My heart stopped. Perhaps they had already overpowered him. Oh, Scipio! You know how long they have been lying in wait for him.

"My blood ran cold, and I hastened to the Kidron. I had to warn him. (No, Scipio, do not look at me like that.) When I approached the bridge, I saw a group of people crossing it. They were singing a song. I thought I recognised his voice, because they say he has a lovely musical voice. I tried to overtake them. When they entered the garden, I was close enough to see him."

"But, Susanna, how could you recognise someone you had never seen before?"

"Oh, Scipio, I would recognise him among ten thousand, because there is nobody like him. But I was too late, for when I tried to enter the garden, someone standing behind the cedar at the gate thrust a spear in front of me. He held his hand over my mouth to prevent me from screaming.

"'What do you want?' he asked.

"'I am looking for Jesus of Nazareth. I want to talk to him.' But he merely laughed and held me more firmly, until another suddenly warned him.

"'Let her be, Romulus! By Jupiter! It is none other than the wife of Scipio, the Bull.'

"Then they let me go, but did not allow me to pass, although I pleaded with them. They said that no one was allowed to enter the garden. 'But you just allowed a group of people to pass,' I said.

"'Yes,' they said, 'but no one else is allowed.'

"So I pretended as though I were leaving, but I did not go far. I hid behind the thick olive trees that grow near the bridge, and waited and watched. I knew only one thing: I had to find him and warn him. Again I crossed the bridge and this time I did not see anyone at the gate, but when I wanted to enter they were upon me and once again I had to turn back. So I crossed the stream higher up and went to stand near the edge of the garden. Everything was quiet and pale by the light of the moon, but I was not afraid, except on Jesus' behalf. And then I thought I heard his voice, and I sneaked closer.

"Underneath the dark shadows of the olive trees I saw people lying. But to one side, someone was kneeling at the winepress, praying, as though he were in the greatest mortal fear. He lifted his head, and the rays of the moon fell on it, giving it a deathly paleness, and I could see large beads of sweat on his brow. I could not hear everything he said. One mournful cry broke the silence: 'My Father, if it is possible, may this cup be taken from me.' There were other words I could not hear, but then he lifted his eyes to heaven and called, 'Let Your will be done!' The words reached my ears on the quiet evening air like a cry of triumph, and I knew that he was the one I was looking for.

"There was something in his face that left me paralysed and speechless with grief. I dared not approach him in his hour of anguish. That holy face, distorted by the agony of death will always be before me.

"The lights in the tents on the Mount of Olives were extinguished one after another, and the campfires died. I could hear the pilgrims sing, and they were so close that I could hear the words of the psalm: 'Our feet are standing in your gates, O Jerusalem.'

"'Oh,' I thought, 'if only I could go to them and bring a large crowd of them to save him from the hands of his enemies!' And then I remembered the small group that had accompanied him. I went in search of them. I walked around the garden on the outside of the broken wall. There I saw three of them (one was Peter, of whom I have told you). They were fast asleep!

"How these people could sleep I do not know, because I know that I would never have been able to close my eyes in the hour of his grief, no, even if it were to last until the end of time. 'Peter!' I called in a muted voice, because I did not want the guard to hear me. 'Peter!' But he was fast asleep, and the moon cast its shadow on the ground, and not a leaf stirred on the branches of the trees.

"Then Jesus returned and touched them and said, 'Could you men not keep watch with me for one hour? Rise. Let us go! Here comes my betrayer!'

"My heart jumped for joy, because I thought that someone had warned him. But it was too late, for while he was still talking, I heard the clanking of metal and saw the gleam of burning torches, while the helmets of soldiers glinted in the light of the moon. The detachment was upon them. I hid behind the broken wall and watched. From the group, one man came forward, like someone who was afraid but nonetheless tried to appear brave. He walked up to Jesus and said, 'Greetings, Rabbi!'

"For a moment Jesus looked at him in silence, and he flinched like someone who had received a slap in the face. Then Jesus said, 'Judas, do you betray the Son of Man with a kiss?' This caused the traitor to recoil, and if the others had not held him up, he would have fallen to the ground. Then Jesus looked at the crowd and said with a soft voice, 'Who is it you want?' And one of them answered, 'Jesus of Nazareth.'

"'I am he,' Jesus told them, and various members of the mob fell to the ground. But the soldiers of the guard approached and arrested him.

"Then he looked at his disciples and said, 'If you are looking for *me*, then let these men go.' The soldiers bound him and led him away, and he offered no resistance as they left the garden. He left on his own, because all of the disciples had deserted him. I followed in the shadows of the trees.

"As we approached the Kidron Valley, where it was much darker, I ran out ahead and went to stand behind the thick cedars. The light of the soldiers' torches fell on the face of the Nazarene as they walked past. He lifted his eyes to heaven, and there in the dark shadows of the valley he said with a sorrowful voice, 'Shall I not drink the cup the Father has given me?' And it appeared to me as if his voice contained both triumph and sadness.

"Once again I followed them, and we passed through the Sheep Gate unhindered. I followed the crowd through the streets and we encountered no one. Everything was quiet as the grave, except for the distant singing of the pilgrims on the hills. 'Oh!' I thought, 'if only we could encounter a crowd of these pilgrims, then the Nazarene may still be rescued.' But the streets were like those of the city of death. The people from the temple had indeed chosen their time well. It was the hour and the power of darkness.

"They brought him to the house of Annas. The soldiers were dismissed, and only the temple guard entered with Jesus. And when the door was shut, I turned away, overcome with sorrow, for I had not succeeded in saving him. It was the hour of midnight.

"On my way home I encountered Peter and John. Peter, big and strong, and used to the storms on the Galilean sea, trembled like a palm tree in a windstorm, and when John saw me, he called mournfully, 'All is lost! Alas! All is lost!' The other disciples have been scattered like sheep without a shepherd. 'Judas has betrayed him.'

"'Is there nothing you can do to save him?' I asked. 'Where are the crowds, those who cut down palm branches and spread their robes before him on the road and shouted "Hosanna!"? You say Judas betrayed him? Do you not know that his enemies do not sleep? At this very moment you are shamefaced, because there in the garden you were sleeping while he was engaged in the bitterest spiritual struggle. Did you not betray him too?'

"'Woman, be quiet!' Peter said. 'Even now we are anxiously on our way to the house of Annas to see what we can do. But we fear that all is lost.'

"Oh, Scipio, is there nothing you can do? Licinius likes you a great deal, and so does the lord Pilate. Can't you do something to save him?"

"Woman, you are ashen and tremble without pause. This Nazarene is driving you out of your mind. If Annas and Caiaphas have a hold of him, Caesar himself would hardly be able to save him. Go to bed now."

I sat there for a long time, deep in thought. I had nothing against this Jesus. I knew what he had done for Bartimaeus, and for Deborah, the wife of Rufus. But I never had much time for people who are obsessed with strange ideas. Such people give the world no rest. To me he was no more than a dreamer of dreams, and during the feast, it is better if such people are out of the way, even if they are completely harmless. Having seen him, I no longer had any fear of war, and I did not, like before, attach value to what the people said about his kingship. Someone like him would never rob Caesar of his throne.

But I was angry about the fact that he had disturbed my domestic peace. Hermas had become estranged from me; Susanna was not herself, and I feared for her mind as well as for her body. And now she even wanted me to save him.

With a curse I went to my room, and there I found Susanna on her knees beside the bed, her face wet with tears. She did not sleep a wink that night, and I slept very little. Every now and then she started like one who is frightened and called his name. Sobbing she mumbled, "Like a lamb he was led to the slaughter. For our transgressions he was stricken."

In my anger I cursed both of them.

Chapter 11

"What is truth?"

I had hardly closed my eyes (or so it seemed to me) before I heard Antonia's trumpet-call, summoning me to report for duty. While hurrying there, I heard the sound of the silver trumpets of the Levites on Mount Moriah. Lambs bleated in the temple courts, and doves cooed in their baskets, all meant to be sacrificed by the priests to satisfy the bloodlust of their Jehovah. When the thick smoke from the burnt offerings in the temple finally lifted, it was as though I had never seen the trees on the Mount of Olives so green and had never heard the birds in the royal garden sing so beautifully as on this joyous morning. Alas! Little did I know what was awaiting me that day.

Rufus was waiting for me at the workshop. "Licinius needs us," he said. "The door will not be opened today."

It did not bode well that all the guards of the fortress as well as all the executioners of our workshop had been instructed to go to the Praetorium. When we in the carpenter's trade were called up, we knew that trouble was brewing. I chose my men carefully. No better team could be found in the entire legion. That was why Licinius had commandeered us. It was still early when we reached the Praetorium; the night watch had been relieved only a short while before.

"What's going on?" Probus asked someone.

"I have no idea. Something concerning the madman from Galilee, it would seem. The temple guard took him to Annas, shortly after midnight. They interrogated him and beat him. They say he will die today. The sooner they kill him, the sooner we will get some peace and quiet around here, if you ask me. I heard that one of his followers had renounced him."

When we marched out, a group of men walked past us, and I saw Rufus's hand playing with the hilt of his sword. "Listen to the Jewish bloodhounds baying for his blood," he said through his teeth. We fell silent. We did not have to be told who the men were who walked past us. Their faces betrayed them.

"By Jupiter!" Varus said. "Did you see the face of that crook, Caiaphas? Did you know that the priests summoned Pilate at this early hour to sentence him to death? I would not give a penny for the life of the Nazarene."

The soldiers from the garrison had to guard the Praetorium, while our team from the workshop had to guard the prisoner. When Licinius gave us the orders, I was filled with wonder about this Jesus; and perhaps I also felt a little fear, when I thought about everything that Susanna, my wife, had told me about him. We stood waiting in the outer court. Suddenly the mumbling of the crowd started to grow louder, until it erupted into violent shouting.

"Look, there he is!" Rufus said, and I saw.

A detachment of the temple guard were making their way through the tumultuous crowd. I saw someone dressed in white, calm in the midst of the angry mob. The pack of vermin snarled and howled. The guard tried to fight a way through that throng of people. Pale and calm he stood there, head held high, as if he did not notice any of the things that were happening around him. Rufus was right when he said that no one could call him a coward.

Finally they reached us. His hands were bound and a rope was tied around his waist. That is how they handed him over to the Roman guard. I put out my hand and took the rope. I stared at him with great interest, because although I had heard so much about him, I had never seen his face, except from a distance. He was weak and exhausted. I wondered how such a man could win the hearts of the people. And then he lifted his head and looked me in the eye – and I knew.

I handed the rope to Quintus and walked behind the prisoner – I have no idea why. Perhaps I was afraid of his eyes. I noticed how firm his tread was, in spite of his fatigue. His outer garment was torn and bloodstained. He was not much taller than most people, and he was slight, although he had a strong build. I wondered whether the rumour that he was only thirty-three could be true.

When we came to a halt, he turned his head, and once again I saw his face. It was whiter than any other face I had ever seen in Judea, and pain and exhaustion were clearly visible upon his countenance. There was blood on his forehead, as if a dirty hand had rested there. His appearance was like that of someone who was worn out, someone who had seen everything of this world that he had wanted to see, and who would not lay down his life unwillingly. His eyes were beyond description, because they shone like stars underneath the pale brow. He lifted his eyes and looked at me; it was as if his eyes burned into my naked soul. Yet they were not stern, but merely serious and sad. And – astonishingly – it looked as if his sadness was not about himself, but about me. I have no idea why – it was a mystery to me – but when he looked at me, I was overcome by an intense longing to throw myself at his feet and to tell him all the things that I have always kept hidden from other people.

Like someone waking from a dream, I heard Licinius command me to take the prisoner to Gabbatha, the place where Pilate's seat of judgement was. I did not stir. Again the command came, and suddenly I felt embarrassed about my weakness. Angry at myself, I grabbed the rope and walked on. The sun shone through the stockades on the tower and gave the hair of the victim a golden sheen.

Dressed in his lavish official robe, Pilate sat down on the ivory throne. The prisoner stood before him. I stood on his right and Probus on his left, while the others fell in behind us. Pilate rose and lifted his hand, calling for silence. Then he turned to Caiaphas and all the priests who were gathered there, and asked, "What charges are you bringing against this man, that you see fit to bring him before me at this unheard-of hour?"

Caiaphas parted his thin lips: "If he were not a criminal, we would not have handed him over to you."

I had been in the company of Pilate many times, and I could see that he was irritated with the high priest. "Take him yourselves and judge him by your own law," he said.

After Caiaphas and Annas had deliberated in whispered tones among themselves, Caiaphas said, "You know full well that we have no right to execute anyone."

"Come!" the governor said, and gestured to us to bring the prisoner to his palace. However, before we could enter, Caiaphas came to Pilate and whispered something in his ear.

Then we entered the palace in the following order: Pilate, the prisoner, Probus and myself. Pilate took the prisoner aside and spoke to him. I could not hear what they were saying, but it looked as if the governor was questioning him. I looked at Probus. The expression on his face was one that I had seen thousands of times on the faces in the arena. It was the expression of a spectator looking at the man that had to face the deadly animal, while he wondered how long the fight would last and whether the game would be accompanied by a lot of bloodshed.

I looked back at the two men, standing to one side, and immediately I got the strange sense that the one in the beautiful robe was the prisoner and the one in the tattered white robe with the bloody brow was his judge. I have no idea why this strange thought should have occurred to me, because the Nazarene stood there with bound hands, and he spoke calmly and quietly. Yet, it appeared to me as if there was something more than mere curiosity in Pilate's manner. Yes, something like deference, almost fear. The prisoner spoke to him in a subdued tone – I don't know what about – and looked at him all the time. My lord Pilate became paler and paler, and eventually turned aside, while biting on his lip. The accused stood still and did not take his eyes from him.

Then Pilate turned back and shrugged his shoulders with a laugh. "Truth!" he said. "What is the truth?" He laughed again, but I noticed that his laugh sounded very hollow, and that his voice was hoarse and forced. Neither did it escape me that he did not look the prisoner in the eye.

"Come!" Pilate said, and they walked past us and went outside.

"By Jupiter!" Probus said. "Did you see? Pilate is afraid of him. I bet you a denarius that he will still cheat the dogs out of the body." We followed.

The roar of a great crowd met us when we emerged from the courtroom. The mob was already four times as large as when we went in. I feared for the peace of the city. Once again Pilate held up his hand, but it took some time before the shouting subsided. And every now and then another murmur arose, like the echo that follows the thunderbolt. But Pilate did not speak before there was total silence.

"I can find no reason to condemn him."

For a moment there was utter silence, and then a roar erupted like the sound of flooding waters. "Away with him!" the call came. "Blood! Blood! Give us blood!" the crowd yelled.

"Crucify him!" one of the priests standing with Caiaphas shouted furiously. "He stirs up the people all over Judea with his teachings. He started in Galilee and has come all the way here."

Immediately Pilate turned to this man and asked, "Is he from Galilee?"

"Yes," the priest answered, "he is a Galilean."

"Then he is under the jurisdiction of Herod," Pilate said. "Take him to Herod, and do not trouble me with him any longer." Without another word he hastily retreated into the courthouse. When he passed me I saw that his hand was trembling.

Chapter 12

The fatal choice

When Pilate decided that the prisoner had to be taken to Herod, Licinius instructed me to take him there, accompanied by a strong guard. I was very glad to have something to do. I would much rather have fought open a path through that throng of swearing creatures, than stand watching the dogs bay for their prey. It was not an easy task to force our way through that teeming crowd, but we accepted it manfully, and more than one filthy, stinking body displayed a bloody bruise where the shaft of my spear had made contact. My eye caught Rufus, to my right, and I saw that he went about his task with no less zeal than I did. They charged at us, swore at us, and fought and shouted, while they tried to get hold of the prisoner, but without success.

"Are you hurt?" Rufus asked when we emerged from the crowd.

"No," I replied with a laugh. A large part of the crowd followed us and continuously swore and sneered, but they did not dare to get within reach of our spears. I was almost sorry that the fight was over. The action had gone some way towards lifting my spirit.

"But you have definitely been hurt," Rufus said, and then I noticed that blood was streaming down my face. My head also felt rather heavy.

"How did it happen?" I asked him.

He laughed and said, "I saw one of those Jewish dogs throw a stone the size of a pomegranate at you. He kept himself hidden behind the others, or I would certainly have dealt with him. Onward, Scipio! To the palace! You have known worse injuries than this." So we arrived at the house of Herod Antipas.

I do not know what happened there, because I was busy tending to my injured head; the blood was running into my eyes, so that I could not see properly. But this I know, when they brought out the prisoner, he was totally exhausted. I had expected little mercy from Herod, and I was not mistaken. Herod and his soldiers had mocked him and spat on him and draped a shiny robe around him. I put out my hand and helped him down the steps and if I had not, he would certainly have collapsed.

Outside the palace the rabble were waiting for us; some ran ahead to the Praetorium with the news that we were returning. Rufus grabbed his spear more tightly and shook it.

"Here we go again, my Scipio!" he said with a laugh. "This time it will be even worse."

I wondered where were the followers of this prophet. Was it possible that they had abandoned him? We did not take the same road back, because we wanted to avoid encountering an even larger crowd and therefore we returned via a detour through narrow streets and alleys. We encountered a group of men and women who were also trying to reach the Praetorium, but to no avail, because their way was blocked by a number of men who drove them back; big, muscular men of the criminal type, probably hired for that purpose. I laughed when I saw a little man on the back of an Ethiopian of roughly my build, trying his utmost to break through the throng. The slave strained forward bravely, while the one on his back hit him with a thick stick he carried with him.

"Minimus is riding Maximus," Probus laughed. "Good shot, little man! Have you ever seen anything like this in the arena, comrades? Look, there goes Bartimaeus. Follow him! Onward!"

It did not take us long to make our way through the throng, because they were careful of our spears and we were rather forceful. Bartimaeus and the little man who had climbed onto the shoulders of the Ethiopian (Bartimaeus said that it was none other than Zacchaeus) broke through with us, but we lost most of the other men and women in the crowd.

When we reached the Praetorium, Rufus accompanied me to the courtroom, so that he could convey Herod's message to Pilate (because the prisoner had been in his care while I had tended my wounds). My lord Pilate had a message in front of him, which he was reading with great displeasure. When we approached him, he pushed it away from him and turned to us.

"I see you brought him back to me," he said angrily. "What did Herod say?"

Rufus gave him the message. I have no idea what happened after that, because after he had read Herod's message, Pilate told me, "Take this to the noble Claudia," and he handed me a sealed parchment.

"You stay here!" he told Rufus. "I want to learn more about this matter."

I went to the palace immediately. Claudia Procula, the wife of my lord Pilate, summoned me to her personal reception room. She was extremely pale, but the jewels on her beautiful body sparkled like the midday sun.

"You are not well, your grace," I ventured to say.

"No, Scipio," she replied with a smile, but she didn't manage to hide her tears. "I am not ill, but I am so disturbed by dreadful dreams that I cannot rest. I dare not sleep for fear that I will dream again." She covered her eyes with her hands, as if she wanted to shut out the daylight.

I have already written how I had saved the life of my lord Pilate, at great personal risk. Since that day everyone in the household of the governor has always treated me with the highest respect. Claudia Procula was favourably inclined towards me, although she was still cold and reserved. I would never have thought that I or anyone else, apart from Pilate himself, would ever see her in tears. I was moved to see somebody like this in such a sad state. I did not know what to say. She turned her back to me to hide her face from me, but I could not help noticing how her entire body trembled.

Suddenly she turned back to me. "Pay me no heed, for I am much perplexed. Return to your lord."

I lifted my spear and walked to the door. "Scipio!" I heard her voice; yet, it did not sound like her voice. She spoke like someone who was overcome by fear. I stopped and turned to her. There she stood with wide eyes and hands clasped to her breast. I saw the rapid movement of her chest. Her breathing was like that of someone who had just run a great distance.

"Come here! I want to learn more from you about this – this Jesus of Nazareth." Her voice was so soft when she pronounced this name, that I could hardly hear it. "Tell me about everything that has happened."

I told her what I knew, and that was gloomy enough. All the while she paced up and down in the room; then with her hands over her eyes, then with clenched fists. It was touching to see how fear and pride tortured her soul.

"And what do you think the outcome will be?"

"Death!" I replied.

She stopped with her hands before her eyes. "Yes! Death! Death! Have I not seen this? Blood! Blood! Blood! Innocent blood on the hands of my lord, Pontius Pilate. On your hands, on mine – crimson blood. Oh! Pontius! My Pontius! You do not know what you are doing!" She pulled her hair; her eyes were wide with fear. "This Jesus is none other than – oh! I don't know."

Exhausted she sat down on the bench. I offered her some of the water that was there, but she declined. Suddenly she got up and walked to the fountain from which the water cascaded. She put her jewel-adorned hands into the marble basin of the fountain. Repeatedly she washed them and then inspected them closely. Then she tried to laugh, but it was more of a sob.

"Scipio," she begged, "save him, I beseech you! Don't allow your lord to pronounce the death sentence. You saved the governor once from grave danger. Save him once again, and this time from an even greater danger. Do this, and Claudia Procula will always honour and respect you." Then she poured lovely red wine into a silver cup and gave it to me to drink, and commanded me to return. "Hurry, Scipio," she said, "because I fear it may already be too late. And, please, for as long as I live, do not tell anyone about my tears." With these words she turned her face to the wall and cried.

I left, stunned and disturbed. I would much rather witness the blood of a man than the tears of a woman. I always thought of her as more than a woman. And yet, she had never appeared more beautiful to me than now, when she was at her most vulnerable.

It was no easy task to find my way back through the tumultuous crowd. When I eventually ascended the steps of the Praetorium, this was what I saw: another prisoner was standing there, heavily guarded, and as I watched, he shouted viciously and wrestled violently with the soldiers. Caius struck him with his spear, and that calmed him slightly. He shaded his eyes with his hands like someone who had just emerged from the dark. Then he took away his hands and looked fearfully at the crowd. Once he had removed his hands, I recognised him as the robber, Barabbas. He was well known to me, as to the entire garrison.

I was not surprised that they had taken him from the cells, because I knew that he deserved the death penalty, and his execution had been put off for too long already. Then Jesus the Nazarene was brought out and positioned next to the murderer. He stood there without saying a word. In the whole of Judea, such guilt, black and vile, had surely never been so close to the purest innocence. These were my thoughts as I saw them there.

My lord Pilate held up his hand for silence. It took some time before the uproar of the crowd was replaced by a murmur – and even longer before the murmur ceased. Then it erupted again, and rumbled on just like receding thunder, but Pilate did not speak before there was complete silence.

"Which one do you want me to release to you?"

It appeared to me that Barabbas knew why he had been brought there, because he broke free from the guard and put out his arms to the crowd and begged them to free him (because during the feast it was customary to release a prisoner for the Jews). He reminded me of a furious beast in the arena – there was foam around his mouth, his arms waved about wildly, and he shouted at the rabble continuously.

The other prisoner did not stir. His appearance was one of extreme calm; he did not say a word, but just watched everything. Then he turned his eyes to the criminal with gentle compassion. And behold, to everyone's surprise the robber ceased his shouting and wiped the corners of his mouth with his rough linen robe. His face changed as if by a miracle. Then he hid his face in shame from the compassionate eyes of the man standing beside him. Humbly he bowed his head, kneeled, and with a cry that sounded very much like a sob, he kissed the seam of the Nazarene's robe.

The guards, who were totally astounded, did not move. The Nazarene laid his bound hands on the head of Barabbas. His lips moved, but no one could hear what he said to the prisoner at his feet. At that moment, had it not been for the priests, the hearing would have been over, and the Nazarene would have been a free man. Caiaphas was the first to break the silence.

"My lord Pilate," he hissed through his teeth, "you gave us the choice. Now release Barabbas to us."

Everything was as quiet as the grave. Then someone behind me said, "Jesus, Jesus of Nazareth. He opened the eyes of the blind – yes, mine too. All of you, also the priests, knew me before as the blind Bartimaeus."

Until that moment I had not known that he was standing behind me.

"Listen, people!" another voice sounded. "This Jesus was my guest. He broke bread with me, and I will give you everything I have if you release him."

I turned to see who was speaking. It was none other than Zacchaeus, still perched high on the back of the Ethiopian. Then the taunting and shouting erupted once again. Furious about this testimony, Caiaphas demanded that the mouths of these men shut. With wonderful calm, Pilate put out his hand to the prisoner and asked, "Why do you hate this Nazarene? Are you not of the same blood?"

Caiaphas responded by crying out even more passionately,

"Away with him!" and the scum of Jerusalem took up the cry. A man with a grey beard took a coin, spat on it and threw it into the air. "Barabbas!" he called. "Release Barabbas to us!"

"Oh, Asher!" a woman cried. "How could you do such a thing? Did not this Jesus heal your wife Abigail when she lay dying?"

Once again Pilate held up his hand, and once again the uproar died down. "What shall I do, then, with Jesus," and while he peered at the prisoner sideways, he continued almost in a whisper, "the one who is called Christ?"

Among the crowd I noticed someone I had taken to be one of the priests. I saw him handing out silver coins to the people. Now he raised his hands. "Crucify him!" he shouted loudly, and when he turned, I saw that it was none other than the rubbish who had come to the workshop as a slave, the one who said that he was from Macedonia. The people who had received the coins from him now also called out loudly, "Crucify him! Crucify him!"

"What!" Pilate said. "Must I crucify your king?"

"We have no king but Caesar!" the priests shouted.

There were many women who begged that the Nazarene should be released, but some of the men silenced them by putting their hands over their mouths. Then it was as if the people shouted with one voice, like the roar of ravenous wild animals: "Take him away! Crucify him!" and the paving reverberated with their wild shouting. Again Bartimaeus started speaking, and before I knew what was happening, the slave who called himself a Macedonian struck Bartimaeus in the face so that blood ran from his mouth. In my anger I grabbed the spy and shattered the bones in his arm. He roared with pain, and I did not see him again. Then I looked at the silent form of the Nazarene. He looked me in the eye and I felt ashamed, I do not know why.

Once again everything was silent. Pilate was speaking. His face was as white as that of a leper, and his voice sounded hollow and strange, which surprised me greatly. I saw how he looked torture and death in the face without blinking an eye.

"Why? What crime has he committed?"

"Crucify him! Crucify him!" howled the rabble. "Take him away!"

A slave brought a silver platter with a basin of water, and Pilate washed his hands in it. The din of the crowd ceased.

"I am innocent of this righteous man's blood; you can see for yourselves." He took the basin of water and threw it to the ground, where it shattered into a thousand pieces. For a moment he stared at it, defeated, and then he turned and entered the courthouse.

"Let his blood be on us and on our children!" and with these words this strange nation took the curse upon themselves.

Pilate summoned me again and instructed me to take Jesus to the city. I was very concerned for this Jesus. I asked myself anew what kind of person he was that everybody either loved or feared him. Never before had I seen anyone like him. When I arrived at the Praetorium again, I saw something that surprised me more than anything I can remember. The hands and feet of the Nazarene were tied to a pillar; his back was bare. I could see that he had been flogged. Jason of the garrison had the whip in his hand and threw it to Probus. Probus took it and struck the prisoner with all his might. I have seen brave men cry when Probus handled the whip, but this man did not make a sound, although he gasped for breath pitifully. Had it not been for the ropes with which he was tied to the pillar, he would have collapsed.

Suddenly a great fear took hold of Probus, so that his strength left him. He hesitated, the whip slid from his hands, and his eyes had a strange glint to them. With a vile curse he bent down to pick up the whip and hit the prisoner even harder. The Nazarene looked at him, and confronted by that compassionate look, Probus lowered his eyes. He turned around and skulked away. I spoke to him, but he did not answer me. I do not know what happened there, but this I do know: that was the last curse that I ever heard from Probus's mouth.

"Enough!" Licinius shouted. "No one will strike another blow, or else you will rob the cross of its burden." But I had the impression that this was not the reason he spoke thus, because he shook uncontrollably.

They untied the prisoner and told him to sit down. Exhausted, he collapsed on the bench, because he had been on his feet throughout that long night. It has to be mentioned here that various men from different countries had joined our ranks shortly before. It was one of them who had spat in the face of the Nazarene; and another of them who saw a thorn bush at the window and took some of the thorns. We watched him, because we did not know what he planned to do. He then twisted together the thorns to form a kind of crown. And then, without warning, he violently pressed it onto the head of the Nazarene.

"Hail, King of the Jews!" he called out.

There was a moment of silence. The blood slowly started running down the pale face. And then there was a loud cry. Probus charged towards the mocker and struck him to the ground. Trembling with fury he bent down over the fallen body. In the silence that followed, the sound of approaching footsteps could be heard. The next moment my lord Pilate stood in the doorway.

"Seize that man," he said, "and tie him up."

Three of the men from the detachment wanted to grab hold of Probus, but he threw them to the ground. Others stormed him, but I pushed them back. "Come, Probus," I said. He looked at me as a child would, and then he put out his hands to be bound. I took him to the cells. Pilate and Licinius followed us.

"By the gods!" the governor said. "I like that big fellow. Keep him locked up until the uprising has passed, Licinius, and then release him. The Galilean did, after all, find one friend." Then he left. I chained Probus.

"Farewell, comrade," I said. "You are a great man."

"I have met one greater than me. Farewell, Scipio." I was on the verge of passing through the door when he called me back. "One more thing, Scipio. Tell Hermas, your son, what happened." And so I left him.

Outside, Licinius was waiting for me. "Scipio," he said, "take Rufus and Quintus with you and go to Golgotha and prepare the place. And when the condemned arrive, see to it that they are nailed to the crosses. Have Rufus and Quintus nail the two criminals to the crosses; you take care of this Jesus."

"No, sir," I said. "I beg you, do not ask this of me."

"There is no one else in this miserable group that I can trust, apart from the three of you. Listen, Scipio! There will be trouble. The dregs of all the nations are trampling one another in the city, and we are completely outnumbered. The men of the legion of Carius, who are coming from Syria, have not arrived, and we have to maintain the peace."

"Sir," I said, "Susanna, my wife, and Hermas, my son, are among the followers of the Nazarene."

"I have known this for some days," Licinius said. "But have you not noticed, Scipio? He is praying for nothing but the courage and strength to forgive his enemies, until death heals the wounds of life." And when he noticed that I was still reluctant, he put his hand on my shoulder and looked me in the eye. "Scipio! You are a Roman, and a soldier of Tiberius!"

Again fate had turned against me. I lowered my head and returned to the rest of my team. He watched me as I walked away. I knew one thing: Licinius himself was reluctant to do the task at hand, and would never allow anyone but me to contradict him. And I also knew this: that day I met two men greater than myself – the one whom I had held in contempt and who was about to be crucified; the other a man I hated, and who was in jail at that moment.

Chapter 13

The hand of a child

We went to Golgotha, the three of us: Rufus, Quintus and I. Varus and Caius, together with the slaves, would bring the crosses to the Praetorium. We were despondent and did not speak much. Rufus began singing a Greek song, but stopped after a few bars. Quintus did not say anything, as usual, yet I knew that he did not approve of the job we had to do.

We reached the place and measured the distances between the spots where the crosses had to be planted. We dug three holes, approximately one-and-a-half ell deep and five ell apart. The earth was hard, because it was very dry. Rufus injured his foot with the shovel, and swore as I had never heard him swear before. I thought about Probus there in his cell and wished with all my heart that I could be there too, because I knew that Hermas and my wife would hear everything – yes, they would perhaps even come to Golgotha.

"What is the matter, Rufus?" I asked. "You constantly look around and stop working the moment someone comes close, and there is fear in your eyes."

"Do you know, Scipio, who saved Deborah, my wife, when the Jews wanted to stone her? I am afraid that she might come here to witness the end. Since that day she has always followed him around whenever he was in the vicinity of Jerusalem. I wish I were far away from here!"

I had almost forgotten how this Jesus had saved Deborah from the hands of the Jews, because no one had ever heard Rufus talk about the matter, and no one ever dared broach the topic in his presence. Truly, our situation was unenviable.

"A soldier is nothing but a servant," Quintus said, "and these things must inevitably happen. Rome commands, but is indeed a harsh master. This Jesus would not have done Rome any harm. His kingdom is not of this world."

We looked at him with surprise. It did not often happen that he spoke this much at a time.

"How do you know?" Rufus asked.

"I saw and heard him, even before he was taken prisoner. He is a righteous man."

"Why crucify him then? What are you doing here?"

"I eat Rome's bread. Rome gave a command. It is good to see a brave man die."

While we were waiting for the victims, we looked out over the orchards of Joseph of Arimathea and the surrounding gardens. The trees were covered with lovely white and red blossoms, and the fragrance wafting towards us on the cool breeze brought tidings of the beautiful days that were ahead – and here we were to plant the tree of death amid this abundance of life!

I rose to my feet. Was I losing all control of myself, as well as all sense of duty? I, who had crucified so many people over the years without any qualms of conscience, could now sense my hands trembling. Had I fallen victim to some curse? I wished by all the gods of Rome that my lord Pilate would rather crucify those evil priests; or set loose his legions on those Pharisees with sword and whip, those whitewashed tombs, as the Galilean called them. I would have been able to cut out the tongues of the filthy rabble without qualms when they vomited their cruel cry: "Crucify him!" I felt that I would surely go mad if this job was not finished soon.

"Scipio," Rufus said, "you are losing your mind. Sit here and drink something." I was extremely grateful for the wine he offered me. Then he took me aside and said, "Scipio, you will kill the body of the Nazarene, but nothing more than the body; for neither you, nor I, nor all of Rome or Judea can kill him, because I see something more than a mere mortal in him." I considered these wonderful words while I watched the gathering crowds.

I had never seen such a throng of people on the hill of execution. The proud and the simple, the corrupt and the righteous, the scoffers and the compassionate were all there. The dignitaries, dressed in purple and fine linen, arrived in their carriages of ivory and gold. There were people from all countries and nations; people of different professions – the shepherd, the water-carrier, the merchant, the priest, the thief, the murderer, the uncouth woman, the virtuous housewife, the innocent maiden, the prostitute – everyone was there to see the torture and death of these men. Many of the commoners of Jerusalem always flocked to the hill for any crucifixion, but it looked as if the entire city had turned out to see this Galilean die. But among all these people I was looking for only two faces – Susanna and Hermas. And whenever a woman with a boy passed me, I trembled. We had our hands full to keep the crowd back. Every now and again we were summoned to clear the way for a dignitary, who attempted to strain through the crowd. All these things I did like someone in a dream.

A group of men approached us, laughing and mocking. "Look," said one of them, a cross-eyed man with broken, yellow teeth, "did not old Jacob lead you to this place? You can trust old Jacob to smell the place of blood from a mile away."

"But where is the Nazarene?" someone in the crowd asked.

"He is coming, and a large crowd is coming with him. But they are making slow progress. We left them behind in the valley below Hezekiah's Pool. He is walking like this," and he put his stick across his back and stumbled underneath it like someone who had drunk too much. His friends laughed and joined in his mockery.

"But we hurried ahead," he said, "because old Jacob must always be as close to the forefront as possible. I have lived in Jerusalem for seventy years, and I have never missed a crucifixion;

but this is a crucifixion like no other," and he roared with laughter, rubbing his hands.

"Look over there!" someone said. "Yes, look!" everyone shouted. They came through the city gates. Licinius rode in front, followed by twenty soldiers of the garrison. We could see the glint of swords, helmets and breastplates. A shout from the crowd announced the approach of the strange procession. And then, louder than the roar of powerful waves, the uproar of the excited crowd walking ahead of the Galilean sounded.

"Take him away!" they shouted. "Crucify him!"

"But look there, Jacob," someone said. "The one carrying the cross is not the Galilean."

"No," various others affirmed, "it is not him."

I looked over the heads of the crowd and my heart jumped with joy. I could see the thieves with their burden, but the one carrying the other cross was not the same person Pilate had given to the Jews. Perhaps they did choose Barabbas after all.

"You fools!" Jacob said. "You will not be cheated, my brothers. Look, there he is, behind the cross. Perhaps they forced that man with the dark skin to carry it for him. And it is better so, because he was exhausted. Now he will last much longer on the cross. You will not be cheated, my brothers!"

The progress up the hill was slow, so slow that it looked as if they would never reach us – yet they crept on. The guards of the Antonia Fortress cleared the way through the crowd, and then I saw the Nazarene. He was indeed exhausted and weak, because he could hardly stand. His clothes were torn; his face, although covered in blood, was as pale as death. His hair was matted with blood and the crown of thorns was still on his head.

A number of women walked next to him, crying, and when they put out their hands to him, as if they wanted to support him, he looked at them with a look of sincere compassion, while he said in a hushed tone, "Daughters of Jerusalem, do not weep for me." A parchment hung around his neck with these words written on it: "Jesus of Nazareth, king of the Jews."

Then Caiaphas followed, dressed in his official robe and surrounded by the temple guards. Behind them came the members of the Sanhedrin and the priests, clothed in white, marching as if they were on parade.

No complaint escaped the dry lips of their victim. He looked at me with a wistful, compassionate expression. When I lifted the heavy cross from the shoulder of the bearer, I knew that, for as long as I lived, those eyes would always be before me.

"Take care of him," Licinius said. I removed his outer garment. He bowed, and I was astounded, because he did something I had never seen any other prisoner do: with his own hands he took off his sandals, perhaps with the idea of making my task somewhat easier. I noticed that his sandals were very worn and his feet bruised, perhaps because of all the long journeys along the poor roads of Galilee.

Suddenly I heard someone shout behind me. A stranger burst through the crowd. His beard and hair were like the snow on Mount Hermon, and his wide eyes looked about him wildly. He had his shepherd's crook in his right hand. He wanted to go to the Nazarene, but the soldiers pushed him back.

"Listen!" he said, with his hands stretched out to Licinius. He flung the two men who held him away from him, in spite of the fact that he was quite old. "Listen! I have gold, a lot of gold."

"Take him away!" the centurion said.

"No," the madman (as he was to our minds) said. "Look here!" From the folds of his clothes, he took a leather pouch and opened it. "Gold! A lot of gold! They call me old Isaac, the Covetous, but they do not know. I come to buy his life. Take the gold, take all of it, and release him. It is the gold of thirty-three years." And softly he whispered, "Thirty-three years since I saw him lying in the manger."

"Your gold is nothing to me," Licinius said. "Rome ordered his death. Get out of here. Your persistence will do you no good." He gave a sign to the soldiers to take him away.

"Then take my life," he shouted. "Let me suffer in his place. My day is almost out, his is only at noon."

Once again the soldiers attempted to take hold of him. He threw his head back. His eyes flashed with anger. With a piercing voice he shouted, "Ephraim! Daniel! The wolves are among the sheep!" and he waved wildly with his stick. The crowd roared with laughter. But it achieved nothing. The soldiers pushed him back and threw him to the ground. Then Jesus looked at him. "The third day!" the shepherd called (because it was the same Isaac Hermas had spoken about). "The third day!" The madness disappeared from his eyes. He tried to get up, and I saw Jacob go to him.

"Come, father," Jacob said. "I will help you," and he put his arm around the old man and helped him to his feet. "Now you can return to your sheep." Jacob turned to his friends, laughing. In his hand he held the shepherd's gold. "Come, father," he mocked. "I will help you. I will carry your burden."

And while the shouting rabble mocked the old man, I swore to myself that I would make sure that his gold was returned to him before sunset.

Quintus had already nailed one thief to the cross. Rufus had his hands full with the other, because he fought like a legion of demons. With great effort and with the assistance of various soldiers Rufus finally succeeded in completing his task. They erected the two crosses and planted them in the holes we had dug. Then there was silence.

"Come on, Scipio, get going!" Licinius said.

The third cross lay before me. The hammer and nails were close by. Once again the Nazarene looked out over the crowd. Then he sighed, and with a wonderful calm he lay himself down on the cross – and waited. For a moment I just stood there as if in a dream, and then I kneeled next to him. A groan of sorrow rose from the crying women when the one they grieved for spread his arms on the cross-beam. I took one of the nails and quickly drove it through the right hand. A shudder went through the body of the convicted, but no sigh or complaint passed his lips. His wonderful self-control caused my hands to shake when I drove the second nail through his left hand. He did not bleed much.

And then I noticed that the wooden block on which the feet

had to rest was fixed too high, and I had no choice but to lower it. I cursed at the mistake. My hand trembled like that of a woman while I was busy with the task. But he did not speak a word. What mortal soul had ever displayed such resignation on the cross? Then, with the hammer in my hand, I took the last nail, and as I was about to put the tip on the feet, a small hand, the hand of a child, crept underneath my hand and positioned itself where the nail had to go through. A small hand rested on my shoulder. I looked up, and there I saw none other than Hermas, my son. With tearful eyes he looked at me and grief-stricken he called out, "Daddy! How can you do such a thing? Don't you know that you are killing Jesus of Nazareth?"

If the dead can feel, I will surely, when I am dead, feel that little hand on my shoulder; and if the dead can hear, I will certainly hear that voice – yes, even then. The hammer slid from my grip. The boy stooped as if to pick it up, but did not touch it. Quintus and one of the women took him by the hand and quietly led him away.

"Daddy!" he called, and there was an indescribable pleading tone in his voice. "Daddy, if you really have to kill him, then also kill this son of yours!" I followed him with my eyes until he disappeared into the crowd. A stern voice startled me: "Scipio, do your duty!"

"No!" I said, and flung the nail down, while I looked at the feet in front of me. For a moment there was utter silence. Then someone giggled; a woman laughed. Livid, I grabbed the hammer and nail. There was a horrified silence when, with a trembling hand, I drove the last large nail through the soft, tender part of the feet. The convicted was now nailed to the tree of torture. Then I threw down the hammer and looked at the Galilean defiantly. His eyes were directed at the place where they had taken Hermas, and were filled with indescribable tenderness and compassion.

Chapter 14

"They do not know what they are doing"

A great silence descended upon the multitudes when four of us lifted the cross and its burden into the upright position. Quintus and Caius lifted the cross-beam, while Rufus and I took the combined weight of the body and the vertical beam upon us and planted it in the hole in the ground between the two criminals. The silence lasted only a moment – then the uproar erupted once again and the spectators continued to taunt and ridicule the man hanging there between the earth and the scorching sun. The upright cross was greeted with a riotous cheer, which was taken up by the crowds on the hills in the distance. The soldiers had their hands full trying to control the noisy throng. The centurion, seated on his horse, moved up and down the line of soldiers, which was continually buckling forwards and backwards. At any moment that line could break under the pressure of the frantic crowd.

It was fortunate for us that another detachment of the legion managed to reach the hill. Their spearheads glinted in the sun as the mob parted to make way for them. In that manner the Roman line managed to hold their own against the crowd.

Rivulets of sweat ran down my forehead as I knelt and wiped my bloody hands on the grass. I remember little of what happened after this. I sat at the foot of the cross and spoke to no one. The scorching sun blazed down upon me; the din of the crowd sounded in my ears; many people walked past me, but I paid attention to no one. I sat there and looked at the droplets of blood dripping from the bruised feet of the Galilean. I don't know why, but I suddenly experienced a great yearning to wipe the blood away. Before I really knew what I was doing, I found myself counting the drops, one by one.

And then I became aware of the presence of someone beside me, staring at me with large eyes. I turned my head and shuddered when I saw a woman standing beside me. She was clad sombrely and a veil covered her face, but behind it I could feel her reproachful eyes resting upon me. She came closer and addressed me in a hushed voice.

"There is blood on your hands. Blood! Blood! Just as I told you!"

"My lady!" I replied, for I recognised her as none other than the noble Claudia Procula.

"Man, I don't know you!" she said. Then she turned her back on me and disappeared into the crowd.

I returned my gaze to the wounded feet. The blood was now dripping more slowly, and oh, how I yearned to wipe away those droplets of blood. While I was still looking, a small hand – the hand of a child – appeared between the nail and the feet. I tried to hear what the rabble were screaming, but above it all I heard the voice of the child: "Daddy, if you have to do this, you might as well kill your son as well."

I closed my eyes. I pressed my hands over my ears. My heart beat like the heart of a mortally wounded man. Someone slipped past me. The stench of his unwashed body filled my nostrils. When I opened my eyes, I saw a filthy rogue spitting on the body of the dying man. He was about to attack a weeping woman kneeling before the cross. Before I knew what I was doing, I was on my feet, grabbing hold of him and flinging him back into the crowd. I went to the woman and offered my help, but she recoiled from me, her eyes wide with fear, yes, with revulsion, so that I, in turn, stepped back.

"Woman," I said, "who are you?"

"I am the mother of the one you crucified." I lowered my head and left. I looked at the soldiers who were casting lots for his clothes, and turned away in disgust. I cast my gaze over the weeping women, and covered my face in shame. I turned my eyes heavenward. The air was hot and oppressive. I looked back at the crowd, and there I saw Bartimaeus approaching, calling out, "Jesus, Jesus of Nazareth! Better you had never opened my eyes! Better for me to have remained blind than to see you hanging on the cross, dying." He tore at his hair like a man possessed.

The Galilean rested his eyes on Bartimaeus, and immediately the man, who used to be blind, grew calm and gazed at the crucified man with a smile. Then, just as the shepherd did shortly before, he whispered, "On the third day," and then he joined the weeping women.

Caiaphas was starting to show signs of great impatience, while the centurion was barking out all kinds of orders. Another priest pointed at the Nazarene with a long finger and shrieked, "Come on, show us a miracle! Save yourself and come down from the cross!"

"In my opinion it is already a miracle," Rufus whispered, "that that old mocker in his white robe still has enough brains to move his tongue."

The weather was muggy and oppressive and the heat unbearable. A hen and her chicks had escaped from someone who had brought them along to be sold. She and her brood fled from among the people, ending up close to the cross. The rabble jeered and threw stones, while the hen tried to protect her offspring under her wings. In a voice of profound sorrow one of the women said, "O, Jerusalem, Jerusalem, how often I have longed to gather your children together, as a hen gathers her chicks under her wings, but you were not willing!"

The mob shrieked and laughed; the hen was lying in her own blood. I looked up at the man on the cross. He was smiling, and there was immeasurably more grief in his smile than in any groan. He looked at the crowd; he looked at the convulsing hen. His lips moved. "Father," he said, and his voice was as gentle as a passing sigh, without any bitterness or reproach; only a long, lingering look in the direction of the priests, the jeering multitude, the centurion. Then, if my eyes did not deceive me, he looked at me and all but whispered (for his voice was fading fast), "Father, forgive them, for they do not know what they are doing."

All the ferocity that I ever harboured in my heart simply crumbled as I stared into the empty blue sky above him, as though I expected to see someone there.

"Father," he said as he lifted his eyes to the heavens – and yes, his eyes clearly showed that he was, in fact, seeing something there. What vision he witnessed with his dying eyes no mortal will ever know. "Father," he said, and I remembered that Susanna said that he was the son of God. Was it possible that this man was truly the son of God? And my hands nailed him to the cross.

My eyes returned to his feet. Again I counted the droplets of blood. Slowly, oh so slowly, they fell on the dark wood – and while I was still gazing at them, the voice of Hermas again sounded in my ears.

Then I heard the muted sobs of the woman kneeling at the foot of the cross. "My son! My son!" she called out. "It is as the prophet wrote: 'Like a lamb to the slaughter.' Thirty-three years have passed since my body was torn, my blood shed for you in that stable in Bethlehem. And now, in your broken body and spilt blood, you bear the sins of the world. Oh, my son! My son!"

Her tears ran in small rivulets down his pierced feet, and with a scarf held in her trembling hand, she tried to wipe the bloodstains from his feet. Then the Nazarene opened his mouth, and while looking at his mother with heartfelt tenderness, he said to the disciple John, who was standing nearby, "There is your mother!" Ever so gently this disciple led the weeping woman back to her people. And immediately a very old woman (whom Rufus recognised as Joanna of Bethlehem), took her place at the foot of the cross and knelt weeping before it.

The time passed unbearably slowly while I watched every movement of that exhausted body on the cross. The face, initially pallid as death itself, turned crimson, and the eyes became glassy. Slowly he turned his weary head from one side to the other, as if he were seeking relief from the pain.

Then the criminal on the right-hand side of the Galilean spoke strange words, words that were incomprehensible to me. Then he turned imploringly to the Nazarene and said, "Lord, think of me when You come into Your kingdom."

With a gentle smile Jesus looked at him and said, "Today you will be with me in paradise."

How wonderful those words sounded to my ears. The murderer spoke no more, but it also appeared as if he had no more pain. And then suddenly the sun was obscured and a great darkness came over the whole land, as if a heavy curtain was concealing the hill from the eye of heaven. The air grew cold and damp as death. A great silence descended upon the crowd; the darkness intensified; everything grew dim. There was no light, except from somewhere beyond the cross, where a blood-red glow seemed to pour through a gash in the black clouds, as if heaven were bleeding. The dim red light was reflected in helmets and breastplates, swords and spears. It traced the outlines of the naked figures hanging there in crimson. The people stared fearfully at one another, and everyone's eyes seemed bloodshot. A piercing cry sounded from the darkness, "My God, my God, why have You forsaken me?"

Never before had the ears of mortals heard a cry like this, and it is unlikely that such a cry will ever again be heard by mortal ears. It filled my heart with fear. It made my skin crawl. I was drenched in sweat, because of the mortal fear that held me captive. I realised that it was the cry of a brave soul; of someone who was more than a mere human being, a King above all kings, whose great heart had just broken.

Despite the darkness, the glassiness of approaching death could now be seen in those eyes that were once so full of sparkle. Time and again bolts of lightning revealed the sorrowful face of the crucified man in stark relief against the dark background. But even during the darkest hour, there was a luminous glow around the head of the Nazarene. His breaths came in fast gasps, and when

when the Galilean women saw that the end was near, they all came up to the cross, and standing around it, they consoled one another with words of love.

The disciple John stood beside me. I could feel his body trembling as he tried to suppress the horrified sobs of his grief-stricken heart. It grew darker still. The blood-red rend in the clouds blazed like fire in the darkness. There was a muted muttering. Somewhere a woman screamed. Others were whispering prayers; but most were quiet. It felt as though even the darkness was breathing. I looked up at the dying man; the light around his head quivered; the writing on the plaque above his head stood out as if written in blood: *Jesus Nazarenus Rex Judaeorom*. The letters burnt their way into my soul.

The darkness grew thicker and blacker; the red light blazed fiercely and more ominously. Slowly the head of the Galilean turned from one side to the other, as though he could see everything. His eyes burned into mine. Then he whispered in a poignant, sorrowful tone, "It is finished." A tomb-like silence prevailed. And then he said, "Father, into Your hands I commit my spirit."

For a moment the silence deepened even more. Then, suddenly, the body strained forward, tense and trembling. A great cry, filled with sorrow and triumph, tore through the silence. His body relaxed; slowly his head sunk to his chest, and I knew that he was dead. At that exact moment the red tear in the sky, which had been diminishing, was completely covered by the clouds. The silence was disturbed by the faraway rumbling of thunder from beyond the adjacent hills. It was as if even the silence became fearful and anxious. Closer and closer the rumbling came. Louder and louder it became, until it was as though the very foundations of the heavens were groaning and shuddering above us. Suddenly it was upon us. The earth trembled and shook, the sky teemed with cries and groans, curses and prayers, and the sound of splitting rocks. For one moment a bolt of lightning illuminated the sky and cast a stark light on the harsh, bare hill with its three crosses. The wind roared over the hill, and the floodwaters of the firmament poured down upon us. And above the clamour of the storm, I clearly heard a little voice: "Daddy, if you really must kill him, go ahead and kill this son of yours as well."

I was lying face down before the cross. When I opened my eyes again, the darkness was fast dissolving. And this is what I saw. There were three crosses standing on the hill. Before them women were kneeling down, weeping. The soldiers were standing around like people who had no inkling of what they were supposed to do. There was no sign of the priests and the masses, except that one could see a crowd of people near the city walls, jostling one another in their haste to get through the city gates. Licinius stood before the centre cross and lifted his spear.

"Surely," he said, "this man was the Son of God."

During the hours of darkness the grieving women of Galilee gathered around the cross, together with Bartimaeus, the old shepherd, and the disciple, whom Rufus recognised as John. This John was profoundly moved, for when he was standing beside me his body was trembling with emotion. He tried to suppress his tears while he spoke words of solace to the Galileans. How it pierced my tortured soul to hear that sorrowful little group speaking words of comfort to one another, standing there in that strange twilight around the body of the crucified man.

Then one of the women went to Licinius and asked his permission to take down the body of Jesus from the cross so that they could bury it. But the one known as Joanna of Bethlehem, who was standing beside the mother, cried in a loud, clear voice, "Even if you bury his body in the tombs; even if you cast it on Gehenna, nothing will hold him. I have seen!" Even as she spoke, the darkness dissipated completely, and the clouds covering the sun disappeared.

Then two of the temple guards came to speak to Licinius. Unsure of what their presence meant, he first guided the women a little distance away. Then he returned to the two guards.

"What do you want?"

"The corpses of the three criminals, so that we may cast them upon Gehenna."

"Who sent you here?"

"Our lord, Caiaphas!"

"Your lord Caiaphas is not my master. From Pilate alone do I take my orders. Go and tell this to him who sent you."

Then another two men hurriedly arrived, and on their heels another one, carrying a heavy package. One of them ran up to Licinius.

"Here is the seal of Pilate!" he said, and handed a letter to Licinius. Licinius read it and handed it back to him with the words: "Let it be so."

Then the centurion ordered us to see to it that the bones of the two murderers were broken, and to ensure that Jesus of Nazareth was dead. And while we were busy attending to these matters he returned to the group of women and spoke gentle words to them, for he did not want them to see what we were doing. Giron pierced the side of the Galilean with his spear. "Look!" he said. "Look at this, comrades!"

This is what we saw. Slowly the blood flowed from his pierced side, but not blood alone, for there was water with the blood. We kept quiet, because we didn't know what it meant.

Then Licinius commanded me to do exactly as the two men instructed. He and the rest of the legion had to return to the city on urgent business. I recognised one of the two as Nicodemus, the rabbi, a man of authority among the Jews. The other was a wealthy man from Arimathea, by the name of Joseph.

I first helped to take down the corpses of the criminals, and then I went to the cross that bore the body of the one that I had crucified. Joseph and Nicodemus did their utmost to help me, but they were not used to doing such work. The mother, and the woman with the white hair who had spoken the words over the body, and two other women were standing at the foot of the cross, watching.

I flung the parchment with the notice written on it to the ground. "King of the Jews," I said to myself. "I have seen no other of the seed of Jacob who is worthy of this name." The crown of thorns I crushed between my two hands, without paying heed to the fact that the sharp spikes were piercing my hands. Carefully I removed the nails that I had hammered in with such violence, and put them into my pocket. With great reverence I took down the body and gave it to the man from Arimathea, as I had been instructed to do.

I have attended the funerals of emperors, kings, monarchs and tetrarchs. I have seen their bodies lying in coffins embellished with jewels, carried on golden biers, accompanied by the lamentations of the eminent and the mighty – but never have I seen tenderness and sorrow as profound as that of the Galileans, when they bore that shattered body down the slope of Golgotha.

I followed them on that wretched road, until we eventually reached the garden of Joseph. We walked along the narrow paths, passing through the quiet and the pleasant fragrances of that peaceful garden. The air was still after the fierceness of the storm, and laden with the scent of innumerable blossoms. The flowers bent their heads, the birds sang beautifully, and the setting sun tinted everything in a golden hue. The tree of death was behind us; the trees of life all around us. Slowly the men carrying the body continued their journey. I could not think of him as someone who was dead.

In front of the tomb – a tomb that had never been used – we came to a halt. On a rocky ledge the mourners lay down their burden and rested for a moment. Someone brought some water and the women started to wash away the bloodstains. Then Joseph called the slave that had followed him and took the burial garment that he had brought along from him. He wanted to dress the crucified man in it, but the woman who was standing next to the mother, she who was called Joanna, fell at his feet and beseeched him, "Joseph the Compassionate, please listen to your maidservant! It was I who heard the first sound of his voice; today I heard the last. His body I first beheld, helpless at birth; today I behold it helpless in death. My hands first wrapped his tender little body in linen cloths; let these same hands today wrap his body in the burial garment." There she lay, weeping at Joseph's feet.

"Mother," he said, as he bent down and helped her to her feet. "I am not worthy to touch his body. You should take care of it."

I turned my face away. I could not bear to witness sorrow as profound as their sorrow – and yet I could not close my ears to their weeping as Joseph read the words of the funeral oration. The roses bent their heads; the trees swayed from side to side in the gentle breeze; the sun set in a sea of blood. In the myrtle-tree a dove cooed in a mournful tone. Overcome with gloom, I stood in that place of tears. I knew that I had no right to be there. Behind me I heard the broken voice of Joanna: "Truly, he took up *our* infirmities and carried *our* sorrows. He was crushed for *our* iniquities – and by his wounds we are healed."

A stifled cry pierced my soul. When I turned around, I saw the mother stretched out over the body of her son. Like a dead woman she lay there. For a moment we could do nothing but stand and watch. Slowly she lifted her eyes to us. She tried to get up, but her strength failed her. With outstretched arms I rushed to her aid. I saw her eyes go to my bloody hands, and with a bowed head I stepped back. I was just about to move away from her, when she stretched out her hand and took hold of mine. When I looked up, her eyes were resting upon me – wide open, beseeching. And yes, I could read forgiveness in her gaze. I bent over and helped her to her feet.

Gentle hands then laid the body of the crucified man in the tomb. One by one the mourners kissed the forehead of the Nazarene, and then stepped outside. I had to stay to oversee the sealing of the tomb. Eventually everyone had left the tomb except for the mother. In the dim light I saw her bending over the body of her son with tears in her eyes. She impressed a kiss on his forehead, and turned to leave. But before she had reached the exit of the tomb, the sorrow of her soul compelled her to come back and kiss him once again. "My son! My son!" she cried. (May God forgive me, I can still hear that voice.) Then, with unsteady steps, she left the tomb, her head bowed. I was left alone with the body of the man I had killed. I went to the entrance of the tomb. There was no one nearby. Like someone about to commit a crime, I was afraid that he would hear me. For a moment I simply stood there, watching the indistinct white shape in the shadows. Then I bent over him and kissed the white shroud. Almost immediately, however, I stepped back in fear and shame, because I realised how unworthy I was. It would be sacrilege for impure lips even to touch such a beautiful figure.

I left that cave of death in great haste and hurried along the deserted path. The sun had already set and the full moon was casting a silver light over everything. I had not even gone fifty paces, when I saw the mother leaning against the moss-covered wall, with her hand pressed against her forehead.

"Please help me," she said. "I am so tired."

I offered her my arm – the blood on my hands burnt like fire – and she took hold of it. No more words were exchanged between us, until we came close to the gate where the other women were waiting for her. Then she looked at me with her mournful eyes and said in a hushed voice, "Forgive them, for they do not know what they are doing."

The two members of the Sanhedrin and the disciple, John, were waiting for me at the gate. They had brought along a few men to help with the sealing of the tomb. When the task was done, we left the garden of Joseph of Arimathea and returned to Jerusalem.

Before we entered through the city gates, I turned around and looked towards Golgotha; stark and grim the three crosses stood there in the light of the moon.

Chapter 15

A Wanderer in the Night

I turned homewards, but before I stepped over the threshold, I first washed the incriminating evidence of my guilt from my hands, so that Susanna and the children would not see it. When I had left my wife earlier that day, she was tired and weak, and her spirit was very disturbed. I had not thought that she would have enough strength to get up that day, and yet I had feared that I would see her on Golgotha. But, I thought to myself, she would have heard everything from Hermas anyway. I went inside the house. She was standing there, waiting for me, her face pale as death itself. I looked into her eyes, and I knew that there was nothing that she did not know. And what was more, there was something in her eyes that filled me with a strange fear.

"Speak, wife," I said. "What is the matter with you?"

She said nothing, but turned around and went into Hermas's room. She beckoned me to come closer. "Look!" she said. The boy was lying there, as pale as his mother. It was piteous to hear him gasping for breath. "My son! My son!" I was on my knees and grasped his little hand in mine. But when I touched him his body trembled with pain. "My son! My son!" I cried out once again. But his eyes were closed, and he did not recognise me.

"Don't touch him," a voice said from behind me, and a woman

removed my hand from the boy. I looked around. It was the woman who had taken Hermas away from the foot of the cross. I had not noticed her until now.

"How did this happen?" I asked her.

"We tried to get him away from there, but he broke free and ran back to the hill. A carriage rushed past at a high speed and the boy fell." She was silent.

"Yes, woman, and what then? What then?"

"Oh, do not ask me that!" she said, and covered her eyes with her hands.

"The doctor! The doctor!" I cried, almost mad with remorse and fear. "Quick, to the house of Atilius, the doctor! Go, Nidia, in haste!" But she did not move. She simply stood there crying, her head in her hands.

"Why do you linger? Run quickly!" And I walked towards her with a raised hand. Susanna stepped between us. I grabbed her by the hand and would have flung her to the ground, but she looked me straight in the eye. "Scipio," she said, and there was something in her voice that caused me to lower my hand. "Atilius, the doctor, has just left here."

"And what did he say?"

She did not reply, but her heart-rending dark eyes looked into mine and told me everything. And then I again heard the voice resounding in my ears: "Daddy, if you must do this thing," (and now the words were different from before), "then you are killing *your* son too." With a curse I turned around and walked out of the room. Susanna followed me and clung to me. "My darling, my darling, where are you going?" she cried, and sobbed like someone possessed by a great fear. But I pushed her away from me and walked away, into the night.

There was blood before my eyes, blood on everything I saw. I craved blood. I had killed him who had touched my heart so wonderfully. He whom I loved more than life itself, I had also killed. He whom I loved more than life itself, was dying. I dared not return to my own home. No other wine but red blood would quench my thirst. I would go to Caiaphas, and to Annas, his father-in-law. I would plunge my hands deep into their cursed blood. The greatest guilt rested upon their heads, and yet they were sleeping on luxurious, perfumed beds, while the taint and the remorse and the curse rested upon me and my house. From deep within my tortured soul I called out to the heavens and shook my fist at the white moon and the stars. In their deathly silence they mocked and taunted me.

I could not stop thinking about the small white face of Hermas as he was lying there with closed eyes on his tiny bed – eyes that did not recognise me. Perhaps death had already come to claim him. Never again would he visit me in the workshop and fetch the adze or the hammer or the axe for me. Never again would he feed the birds in the courtyard, or play with the sword and shield that Rufus had made for him. Never again would his childish chatter bring joy to my ears and heart. I thought of many things that would seem like trifling details to anyone else, but were to me like the breath of life itself. And time and again I saw his little hand before me and heard his small voice in my ears.

I stumbled along blindly, without knowing where I was going. Suddenly I lifted my eyes and saw three crosses before me, stark and grim in the moonlight. Behind me was the city. The moonbeams cast a soft light on the temple and the synagogues that had been erected for the service of Jehovah. And on this Golgotha someone had been crucified whom the priests of that same temple had condemned to death. I came to a standstill. What miraculous coincidence had led me there I did not know. I was standing before the cross to which I had nailed an innocent man. An innocent man! And I remembered everything that I had heard about him; how some in the workshop spoke of him as someone completely different from other people; a prophet of whom the holy men of old spoke; the chosen one among the Jews; the righteous servant of their Jehovah. Everything I had ever heard – and that I had barely paid heed to – resounded in my ears. Perhaps he was more than a mere mortal! No child of man that I had ever met was his equal.

And then I remembered (and how strange that I had not thought of this before) the words of Licinius: "Surely, this man was the Son of God." The Son of God! And it was my hand that killed him! If Licinius's words were true, then I, Scipio, had committed Deicide, for alas, too late, too late, had I understood that the one I had crucified was *the Son of God.*

I thought of Pilate and of Claudia, his wife, of Probus, and everything that had happened there. I thought of the darkness, of the earthquake, of the blood-red tear in the sky. I thought of the crucified man's incredible cry before he died. Truly, he was more than a mere human being! And I cast myself down before the cross and threw my arms around it. It was cold to the touch, and damp from the dew of the night. I raised my voice and cried out from the terror of my soul, "Jesus of Nazareth – Son of God (for this is what Licinius called you) – you whom I have crucified! Hear me if you can! It is I, Scipio Martialis, Scipio the Roman. The same Scipio who drove the nails into you now calls upon your name. Take my life, I beseech you, destroy me if you wish. But he, my son, that same Hermas who tried to save you, Hermas who loves you more than all the things of this world, I beseech you, spare his life. Do not hold him accountable for my sins. Crush me, destroy me! But I beg of you, spare him!"

I lifted my eyes, as if hoping to see him there on the cross, but all was quiet and pale in the moonlight – the cross was empty. "He probably cannot hear me," I thought, "because he is lying in the garden of Joseph. I will go there and pray to him." I left the hill and went to the garden of peace and rest. I followed the narrow path until I reached the tomb. I kneeled alongside the tomb, where I could hide behind the rosebushes, and spoke in a soft voice: "Jesus, I beseech you, please pay heed to me! Destroy me and kill me, but please spare my son Hermas! He is dying – he is so young still – everybody loves him so, and he loves you. Please do not take him from us, I beg of you! Let your vengeance come upon me, Scipio! O crucified one, with your last breath you begged the Father to forgive your enemies; and even though I do not know why you were allowed to die, I want to make this oath: never again will this hand nail someone to the tree of death, for I now believe that you are the giver of life, and that you alone have the right to take it away."

I leaned against the wall of stone that separated the living from the dead. The peace of the garden flooded my soul. No longer did I hunger after the blood of Caiaphas. I desired nothing, except for the life of my son Hermas.

"Spare him, I beseech you," I prayed. "Strike the father down, but do not take away the child!"

For how long I remained kneeling there I do not know. The silence and the peace were like a balm upon my weary soul, and the cool evening breeze cooled my feverish brow. The moon was shining brightly and the flowers looked as if they were made of silver. Perhaps he had heard my prayer. Then I glimpsed the glow of torches. A band of men entered the garden. I concealed myself among the shadows of the trees and watched from there, for I did not want to be seen at that moment, nor did I want to speak to anyone. From within my hiding place I recognised several soldiers from the legion as well as a few temple guards, and satisfied that they were not robbers, intent on breaking into the tomb, I quietly made my way out of the garden.

I desired no rest or food or drink. I simply wanted to be alone in the night to carry out a strange desire that had come upon me. I was barely half a mile from the garden of the rabbi when I heard the screeches of the night birds. I knew all too well what the sound meant, for I had witnessed the orgies of the vultures on many a battlefield. The dreadful creatures were of course now tearing to pieces the corpses of the crucified criminals. Up until that moment, the dead body of a human being had been nothing more to me than carrion for the jackals or other beasts of prey.

However, when I thought of the Galilean lying peacefully in the tomb, I suddenly felt that it was my duty to bury the bodies of these men. At the same time I was amazed at the feeling of compassion that arose within me, for I had often been told that the heart of Scipio was as hard as stone. Cautiously I proceeded to the place to which the slaves had dragged the corpses. There, on the communal grounds, the ghastly shapes lay, their faces so distorted that I could not tell the two corpses apart. Their eyes had also already been pecked out by the birds.

How badly I wanted to know to which of these two men's spirit the promise was given that he would be in paradise with Jesus this day. I was overcome by a profound tenderness towards them, and I nearly uttered out loud my hope that their spirits had not been separated, regardless of where they had ended up. One after the other I carried the bodies to a deep chasm in the rock. I was forced to use a big branch to drive away the screeching, bloodthirsty birds. I cut down green branches from the overhanging trees and used them to cover the corpses. Then I piled a big heap of stones on top of the branches to protect the bodies from the birds and animals.

After I had completed my task, I was struck by the thought that the all-forgiving one would have been pleased had he known that those who had been crucified with him had found a grave.

I left Gehenna and wandered around in the darkness, not knowing where I was going. The wind rose, and big clouds covered the moon, but I stumbled on. Earlier, when I had knelt at the foot of the cross, and again when I was at the tomb, a wonderful peace had overcome my being. But now that I once more felt myself far removed from his presence, my mind was in turmoil.

The priests maintained that this rabbi was not the Messiah, that he was a trickster and a fraud. If the priests were right, then there had never been a trickster with a face like his; and never had a man died as he had died. I was nothing more than an ordinary soldier of Tiberius, and I tried to console myself with the thought that I had simply obeyed the orders of Rome. And yet I could not forget how Caiaphas and his father-in-law, Annas, had persecuted this righteous man unto death.

Jerusalem lay a short distance away, peaceful in the soft light of the moon, and beyond the walls, the dome of Solomon's temple could be seen clearly against the dark blue sky. Further into the city the luxurious palace of the high priest could be seen, and while I was looking at it, I once again heard his hate-filled cry, "Take him away! Crucify him!" Caiaphas, the high priest, who had persecuted the Nazarene unto death – the Nazarene, who might just be the Son of the Almighty in whose name this temple was built. I do not know why they killed him. Rufus had heard the Nazarene saying to them, "You snakes, you brood of vipers, how will you flee from the coming wrath?"

Once again I was filled with an overwhelming hatred, yes, a thousand demons spurred me on. I was thirsty and I thirsted after the blood of those worthless priests whose religion had become nothing but a putrid plague to me. Whether he who was lying there in the tomb, was still able to exercise his influence over me I don't know. But this I know: his words came to me from somewhere in the night, because I remembered the prayer that Susanna had taught Hermas (she called it the Lord's prayer), "Forgive us our debts, as we also have forgive our debtors." These strange words struck me as truly wonderful, for we legionaries knew nothing of forgiveness. And now this prayer, as it sounded from the mouth of a child, tempered my murderous urge. I had taken one life already, the life of someone who prayed for his enemies even when dying. It would not please him if I were to take another life in revenge.

I did not care where I went that night. I have a vague recollection of being in the valley of Hinnom and passing through the valley of Kidron. I seem to remember standing, shivering, under the olive trees of Gethsemane and then slipping out through the small gate. I stumbled along until I came close to the grave of Absalom. Only then did I realise that the moon had already disappeared from the sky, and that a new day was on its way. In my selfish sorrow, I had left my son and my grieving loved ones alone at home.

Filled with remorse, I immediately turned back home – and there before me I saw something the likes of which I had never seen in all my years. What it was I could not immediately see, and I did not particularly care to find out. I had only one goal before me, and that was to get to my son. And yet I could not tear myself away from the dreadful thing that looked vaguely like a human figure. Upon closer inspection, I saw the body of a man. He was hanging from a rope tied around his neck. He was dead, and in the dim light of dawn, I recognised the face as belonging to someone I had seen before. Those fixed, staring eyes were those of Judas – Judas Iscariot. For a moment I just stood there, unable to move. The morning breeze started blowing softly; the rope creaked; his robe moved slightly; gently the body swung towards me. The full brilliance of the breaking day fell upon the ghastly face. I turned around and fled the scene as fast as I could.

"Halt!" It was Galatius of the guard, but when he saw who it was, he stepped aside and allowed me to pass. I spoke no word, but simply walked past him, into the city. Cold terror followed on my heels. Why I was so overcome by something like this, I don't know, for death had always been my brother-in-arms. I had buried the ghastly corpses of the criminals at Gehenna without any feeling, except for a strange sensation of pity and compassion. But there was something in that twisted face in the cold, pale light of dawn that – no, God! Not even now, do I dare to put it into words here.

I returned home like a bird to its nest. Against the wall, beside the door, a white figure was leaning. Susanna was waiting for me. Like a drunken man I stumbled towards her.

"Thank God you have returned!" she said. Her voice sounded as though it were coming from very far away. She sat me down on the bench and put a cup of warm wine to my lips; but I almost couldn't drink it, for my breath was coming in fast, shallow gasps. When I was told that the boy was sleeping, I closed my eyes. The sun was already high in the sky when I awoke.

Chapter 16

Hermas goes home

Susanna leaned over me. "Get some rest," she whispered, "while I quickly prepare a meal for us."

I got up, completely bewildered. Why was I lying on the bench fully dressed, so late in the day? I passed my hand over my forehead; the scent of dried blood clung to it, the blood of Gehenna, and then I remembered everything. Here I was lying in the house to which I had sworn never to return. Only a door separated me from the mangled body of the boy whose blood was on my head. And she who had brought him into this world with the pain and sorrow of labour, was serving me with the greatest tenderness and looking at me without the slightest sign of reproach. Truly, I thought, the love of the followers of the Nazarene cut much deeper than the sword of revenge. If only she would curse me and heap reproaches upon me; if only she would turn her back on me! But she did nothing of the kind. Instead, she merely served the meal.

"I can't eat," I said, and pushed the plate away from me.

"Come, my husband," she said, and put her cool, soft hand upon my brow, while smiling at me as in the days before our engagement. I ate little of the food, and I could not bring myself to speak a single word. She left me and went to Hermas's bedroom. I was burning with desire to know how the boy was, and yet, I feared her return. It seemed like a very long time before the door opened and she appeared again. Slowly she came towards me.

"Scipio," she said, "he is calling for you."

"Wife, how can I go to him? How can I look him in the eye? His blood is on my head, and I killed the one he loved."

"No, Scipio, do not fear. He recalls nothing of all that has happened, since the day he and that young Samuel met the Christ in the marketplace. He has partial memory loss. Do not fear!"

I went to his room. There he was, pale and weak, and his dark eyes were large and extraordinarily bright. I sat down beside him.

"Daddy," he said, "why did you stay away so long? I was calling for you all through the night. Where were you?"

"I was on a journey, my son." He put his little hand in mind, as was his habit.

"Daddy, there is blood on your hands. Was there a riot?"

"No, my child. I had to take away two criminals who had been executed."

For a while he was silent. Perhaps he found speaking painful. Gently I put down his little hand and ran my hand through his hair. He looked at me as if there was something that he could not comprehend.

"Daddy, what is wrong? Why are you so quiet? Why are you looking at me so strangely? Your hair also looks funny, all ashen. Are you ill?" (Up until that moment, I had not known that the hair on my head had turned completely grey.)

"No, my son, but there are things that trouble me, and I am very worried about you."

"Daddy, but what is wrong with me? I am so tired and I can hardly move. Mommy can't tell me anything."

"Don't worry, my son. Soon you'll be well again. You'll come to us in the workshop again. You'll play in the fields and pick flowers; you'll run around in the hills and swim in the dam."

"I'll go to the temple and look for Jesus. He is in the city, because I have seen him and spoken to him. Daddy, will you come with me? I know you won't be able to keep yourself from loving him too."

"Yes, my child."

"But Daddy, I can't walk. What should I do?"

"I will carry you in my arms, until we find him. But don't be afraid, you'll grow strong again." I was unable to speak another word. He was quiet again for a while. Gently I stroked his hair. Then he turned his head and looked at me.

"Daddy, there is something that Jesus said that I haven't told you yet. At first I didn't pay any attention to it, but now it is bothering me. I don't know what it means. When he left, after he had spoken to Samuel and me, he said to Peter: 'The day is near when people will all forget their hatred and stand weeping around my crushed body.' Daddy, what did he mean by his 'crushed body'?"

I turned my head away. I simply could not look into those searching eyes. He put his little hand into mine once again. He tried to lean over towards me, but a sudden stab of pain forced him to lie back.

"Daddy, tell me, is my body crushed? I can't sit up. I can hardly move at all. Tell me, Daddy!"

"You'll soon be well again, my child. You have to rest now, because you are tired."

"I have such beautiful dreams, Daddy. I see the manger, and the oxen, and old Isaac, and Mary the mother, and the child Jesus. I see them all, Daddy."

"That's wonderful, but now you must rest, my little boy. I will stay with you." He closed his eyes. His chest rose and fell ever so slightly; it looked as if he was almost not breathing at all. I leaned over him and kissed his little white face. "O Jesus, crucified one," I prayed, "please spare his life, and in my arms I will carry him, even to the ends of the earth." I kissed him again, and then went out of the room. He smiled in his sleep.

It was the time of the midday meal when I stepped into the workshop again. When I came to the door I heard the muted voices of my comrades, but they looked up and fell silent when they saw me. I took my adze and worked by myself. I had no desire to speak to anyone, and all the time the image of Hermas was before my eyes. His face was pale and incredibly beautiful, his little chest went up and down as he breathed, and he smiled in his sleep. The sun shone warmly on the workbench. The men were talking to one another in hushed voices. The atmosphere was filled with the sounds of everyday labour and the pleasant fragrance of the timber. In silence I worked at my job, and a kind of dull, painful peace took possession of my soul. As if in a dream, I again heard the words the boy spoke as he was leaning over towards me: "Daddy, tell me, is my body crushed? I can't sit up; I can hardly move at all." Then he was asleep again. His little head was lying on the cushion and his curls were hanging loose. One tiny hand was stretched out on the blanket, and the other was lying on his chest, where it gently moved with his rhythmic breathing. And then I felt a hand on my shoulder. I looked up. It was Rufus.

"Come, Scipio," he said.

I looked at him with utter bewilderment. Then I realised that the sun had already sunk low in the sky, and that the others had long since left. I got up and left like a sleepwalker. Probus was waiting for me at the gate.

"I have to go past your house, Scipio," he said. "May I walk with you?"

"Yes."

We walked some distance without speaking. He looked extremely uncomfortable. Finally he said, "Scipio, I've heard everything about little Hermas. How is the boy?"

"Fine. When I left home he was sleeping."

Again we walked in silence for a while, and then he said, "I made him something. Look at this!" He showed me a tiny shepherd's crook, the size of a man's middle finger, and a sheep, and a small manger, all cut from wood. He looked at me shyly and blushed like a young girl.

"You know that the boy often spoke to Bartimaeus about these things, and I have no child of my own." Then he opened the bag that he had with him, and showed me the gifts made by all the other carpenters.

"You see, we all heard what had happened, and we all love him – yes, even I who hit him that day. While lying in my cell last night, I thought about him a great deal."

I came to a sudden halt. I had been so caught up in my own sorrow that I had completely forgotten that Probus had been thrown in jail. And now he was walking here beside me.

"But you," I said, "how did you get here? I left you in jail."

"Yes! But this morning they opened the doors and released me. Licinius spoke a few words to me about the kind of behaviour that behoves a soldier, but I did not pay much attention to what he was saying – and I don't think he was particularly bothered either. After that he gave me something to eat and sent me back to the workshop."

I suddenly remembered what Pilate had said, and I understood the matter. By this time we had reached the door of my house.

"Come inside, Probus," I said. "You can see the child with your own eyes." He hesitated on the threshold, as if he was afraid to step inside. Yet I realised in my heart that he had walked with me in the hope that I would invite him in to see the child. Never before had I seen him so shy, timid almost. Together we went into the house.

"Is he well, Susanna?" I asked.

"He is resting," she said. "Mary the mother, and Joanna of Bethlehem were with him while you were away. They witnessed what he had done there on Golgotha, but they only heard at about noon today what had happened on the highway. They sat with him a long time and consoled him. I asked them not to talk to him about – about what happened on Golgotha. He remembers nothing of what has happened since the day he saw Jesus in the temple."

We went to his room. His eyes sparkled brightly with joy when he saw me. Oh! If he had to remember everything those eyes of his had beheld, how would I ever again be able to look into them? I recalled the compassionate expression in the eyes of the Nazarene when Quintus and the woman lead the boy away. Perhaps he who had opened the eyes of the blind, could close the eyes of the memory to the things that Hermas had seen.

"Daddy," he said, "Mary, the beautiful mother, and Joanna with the silver hair were here to see me. They told me again about his birth, and about the stable in Bethlehem, and so many other things that I did not know about – so many wonderful things, Daddy. Oh, Probus! Is that you hiding behind Daddy? Did you also come to see me?"

"Yes, my child. I came to wish you a speedy recovery."

"I am really glad to see you. Sit there with Daddy, so that I can see your face."

"Are you in pain, my son?" I asked him.

"Not if I lie still, Daddy. But I am so tired and all I want to do is sleep the whole time. And when I sleep I see *him* in my dreams."

"Then sleep, my child, sleep, for then you will get better quickly."

"No, I don't want to sleep now, because you are here with me. Daddy, did you see Jesus today? I know that he is in the city, because I saw him at the temple. If you see him, you should tell him about me, so that he can come here and heal me."

"Yes, of course, my son."

"Yes, Hermas, my child," said Probus, and with these words he turned away, his big form shaking with sobs.

"Do you still mock him?" Hermas asked, with an expression of quiet reproach in his eyes, because of course he did not know what had happened. Probus stared at the child for a long time, with a wistful expression in his face. Then he said, "Hermas, my son, I have fought the Galilean for the last time, and he has won – not by the power of the sword, however, but by the power of his all-forgiving love. Do you know that lepers went to him among the tombs, and that he touched them and purified them? Hermas, I'm telling you, in the same way, Jesus touched my impure heart and purified it."

I looked at Probus with astonishment, because I was surprised to hear such words coming from his mouth. Then Hermas put his little arms around Probus's neck. "Will you bring Jesus to me?" he implored. Probus lowered his head, because he could not tell the child that the Galilean was dead.

I could not witness the scene any longer, and got up and went to the door. "There is something that Probus wants to tell you, Hermas," I said. "I'll be back shortly." I went to Susanna.

"Wife, the child doesn't have much pain. Do you think that it is possible that Atilius, the doctor, was mistaken?" (And I thought back to my prayer in the garden, but I was too shy to speak about it.)

"Atilius was here an hour ago. He says before the sun sets tomorrow ..."

I collapsed onto the bench. I could hear the voice of Probus, softer and gentler than I had ever heard it before, and the eager chatter of Hermas. It appeared as though Probus had lost all fear now that the two of them were alone. I heard him trying to bleat like a sheep, and I heard the boy laughing heartily at his attempts. It seemed so strange to me that he who was chattering and laughing so cheerfully at that moment, he who had up until then not known anything of illness or pain or wounds, would be lying there the next day, cold and still in the sleep of death. And the one who would have been able to save him and to give him back to me was already in the grave – and it was *my* hands that drove the nails.

I returned to the room. The child was sleeping, with a smile of joy on his face. One tiny hand clutched the small, carved manger, while the other was lying in the hand of Probus, who was sitting beside the child with a bowed head. Slowly the tears ran down his face that bore the scars of so many battles, and slowly they trickled onto the blanket. He looked up at me, without even trying to hide his sorrow. As gentle as a woman, he slipped the little hand from his, and pressed a kiss on the brow of the small martyr.

"Farewell, my brave little man," he whispered, as we quietly left the room. We had supper together: Susanna, Nidia, Probus and I. We did not speak much, for our hearts were filled with pain and sorrow. Probus had to leave almost immediately after the meal, because Licinius had ordered him and Rufus – and a few others – to guard the sealed tomb in the garden. By that time almost everyone in the city knew that the seal of the Sanhedrin had been placed upon the tomb.

A sealed tomb! While thinking about the armed guard placed before the tomb, I asked myself what would have happened if no one had asked to take the body of the Nazarene, and it had simply been thrown on the communal grounds to become carrion for the vultures? Would the priests have placed a guard at Gehenna? Would the birds have torn his flesh apart, or would his Father have restrained them? While I was pondering these thoughts, Probus asked Susanna, "Do you think that the Galilean will be raised from the dead on the third day?" He was speaking in a low tone. There was a tender, longing expression in his eyes while he listened to Susanna's words of faith and hope. To me her faith seemed foolish and futile, for I had seen the wounds in his hands and feet, his tortured back, and the terrible wound in his side. I was certain that he was dead. When Probus left on that day of the Jewish Passover, the sun was already setting.

"Tomorrow," he said, "is the third day, and regardless of whether he is raised from the dead or not, I believe that he is the Son of God."

I accompanied him to the door. We embraced each other. "Oh, Scipio, Scipio! If I had someone like your Susanna as a wife, and a son like your Hermas, I would not have been the man you know today. You didn't know me when I loved Lavinia. But she is dead. The grave claimed her as its property many years ago, when I was still young." And with these words he walked into the darkness without looking back at me, but I thought I heard the sound of a strong man almost choking in his effort to suppress a sob.

As the evening wore on, the boy's condition worsened. He was distressed and restless. He spoke of many things, but did not always know what he was saying. Sometimes he was in the stable in Bethlehem, then he was with Samuel in the marketplace, while Jesus was talking to him.

"Did you hear, Samuel," he once said, "He says he'll see me again soon, someplace far from here." Another time he exclaimed, "Oh Jesus, do not delay much longer! I am waiting for You, and I grow so tired, so very tired."

An hour before midnight he dozed off, but his sleep was restless.

Susanna sat with him and it seemed to me, counted his every heartbeat.

"Scipio," she said, "he is sleeping. You should also get some rest – you are exhausted. I will stay and keep watch over him."

"But wife, what about you? You haven't slept a wink since they brought him in here from Golgotha. Let me stay here with him."

"No, you are only a man. It is not a man's work to keep vigil. I will call you if it is necessary."

I lay on the bench that stood across from the east-facing window. Still my eyes could see the little chest barely moving, and the mother's tense, pale face was still before me. And with these images clear in my mind, my eyes closed and I fell into a restless sleep.

It was daybreak when Susanna leaned over me and awakened me. "Scipio, come! He is calling for you."

I jumped up and went to him. He was lying there with his little arms stretched out on the blanket. "Daddy," he said, "please lift me up."

I lifted him, and Susanna fluffed and reorganised the cushions behind him. Large droplets of sweat formed beads on his forehead. His cheeks were on fire, and his eyes sparkled with a wonderful light.

"Daddy, Mommy, Nidia!" he said. "Just listen to the wonderful dream that I had. I was in a garden, and there were so many trees and roses and lilies and other beautiful flowers. I could smell the blossoms too. Beautiful coloured birds were singing in the branches of the myrtle-trees. Everything was sparkling in the light of dawn.

Then the sun rose over the hills, and there before me I saw a cave cut from the rock. Inside the cave someone in white clothes was lying. He was sleeping, with his arms folded on his chest. The sun climbed higher in the sky, and its rays fell on the face of the one sleeping there. I could not take my eyes off that face, because it was the face of Jesus – the same face that I saw at the temple. Then an even greater light shone on his face, and he woke up and looked at me with a smile. He called me by my name and said, 'Hermas, my child, I have passed through that valley that people call death, and shortly I will leave this tomb and ascend to my Father. I want you also to go to him, because by your faith and your sacrifice you showed that you love me.'

"Then I said, 'Oh Jesus, I so much want to go with You, but I am so ill, and I cannot walk.'

"'Then I will carry you against my chest,' he said.

"And Mommy, I am so glad that I am wearing clean clothes, for I know that he will be coming soon."

He fell quiet and closed his eyes. Very softly he breathed, so that it almost appeared as though he was not moving at all. We waited, for we knew that the end was near. The first morning light fell over the hills. It illuminated the room with a brilliant light, and circled the child's head with a halo of gold.

"Look!" he cried, as he tried to sit up with eyes wide-open. "Look, he is standing by the door! He is waiting for me. You probably didn't see him, Mommy, or you would have invited him in. Jesus! Jesus! I am coming, I am coming!"

Softly he leaned his head against the bosom of his mother. With a smile he closed his eyes and fell asleep. And in his sleep he ceased breathing.

We stayed like that for a long time. Nobody said a word. Nidia sobbed softly; the mother held the child as if she was afraid to disturb him in his sleep. I was amazed; I couldn't bear to see them like that. Slowly I turned my eyes to the window on the east side and looked at the daybreak. The sun steadily rose and chased away the morning mist. The light clouds were fringed with red and lay like sleeping seashells in a blue sea. Jerusalem lay bright and white in the morning light; the healing rays of the sun warmed the city and coloured the room in orange-red.

The glory of the sun in the east slowly awakened the city to a new day. I could hear the sound of music on the hills; footsteps sounded in the street. Somewhere a bird called his partner. In the glow of the new morning, everything looked fresh and happy – everything, except the silent white figure that was kissed by the sun, but didn't awake, all except those that sat in the room with their heads bowed.

Chapter 17

The third day

From the street came the sound of a multitude of footsteps and the voices of people calling out to one another, "He has risen! He has risen!" Someone came to our door and knocked softly but urgently. We looked at one another. No one moved, and Nidia did not cease her quiet sobbing. Another knock was heard, and then the door slowly opened.

"Susanna! Susanna! He has risen!" a woman's voice called triumphantly – and then Mary, the mother of Jesus, and Joanna were standing before us. They stared at us in quiet bewilderment. Then Mary, the mother, quietly went to our little boy and impressed a kiss on his white forehead. Joanna with the silver hair followed her example. At this, the stoic sorrow of the child's mother dissolved and the tears started to flow. She had not shed a single tear from the day of the tragedy up until that moment. Joanna picked up the child and laid him on the bed, while Mary tried to console Susanna. They took out spices and precious perfumes, and started to anoint the body.

"Did you know that the boy would die?" Susanna asked. "How else did you know to bring the spices here?"

"No, Susanna," Mary said. "But a wonderful thing has happened, and I would very much like to tell you about it, but I don't want to intrude upon your great sorrow."

However, Susanna insisted that she wanted to hear everything, and so Mary proceeded to tell us, "Early this morning, when it was still dark, we went to the tomb in the garden. But before we had reached the tomb, Mary Magdalene, who had gone ahead of us, came running back to us, crying, 'He has risen! He has risen!' Pale and trembling she told us how she had come to the tomb and had found it to be empty. We hastened ourselves to the tomb, and lo and behold, it was just as she had said: the seal had been broken and the stone before the entrance had been rolled away."

'Did I not tell you there on Golgotha that death would never be able to hold someone like him in its grasp?" Joanna cried.

"But why did you come here?" Nidia asked. "Did you perhaps expect to find him here with my little brother?"

"We did not know where he went," Joanna answered. "But I recalled how Hermas had called for him, and I thought perhaps he had come here to see the child."

"And indeed he was here," Susanna said. "Hermas saw him before he closed his eyes. But our eyes were veiled, so that we could not see him."

"The spices that we wanted to use to anoint my own son," Mary said, "we have put on the beautiful body of your son, because he is worthy of it."

For a while they remained sitting there in the death-room, sometimes moving about quietly as they anointed the little body. I paid no heed to the words of comfort that Mary, the mother, and Joanna showered upon me. All that I knew was that he whom I loved more than anything else in the word was lying there – dead. And my heart grew cold and stony within me. I had prayed to this Jesus of Nazareth – I, Scipio the Roman, who had not prayed to any other god since I had taken up the sword. Kneeling at the foot of the tree of death, and at the tomb in the garden of Joseph, I had prayed to him in the greatest agony of the soul – but he had mocked me. The one who had loved life was dead; the one who had sought death was still alive. Truly, the curse rested heavily upon my house and me.

Then Susanna rose and pressed a kiss on the brow of her son. He doesn't even know about the kiss, I thought to myself, and she can't wake him from his sleep anyway. The other women also kissed him. And when Mary of Nazareth leaned over him, I said to myself, "It's easy for her to speak words of comfort, for her son is alive."

Then Susanna came to me and said, "We are going out to make arrangements for the funeral. Farewell, Scipio. Be of good courage!"

I knew that her heart was broken, despite her cheerful words. I did not move – I did not even look at her. I simply sat there, with my eyes fixed on the body of my son. She hesitated for a moment, as if she wanted to say something more, but then she turned around and left the room with Nidia and Joanna.

Mary, the mother, placed the flowers around the body, and then she came to me. She put her hand on my arm, just as she had done there in the garden, and softly she spoke my name, "Scipio!" I did not answer. "Scipio!" she repeated. "Do not harden your spirit, I beseech you. I know very well what you are feeling in your heart of hearts, and it is right that you should grieve. Three days ago my son was lying dead, and I thought that my heart was broken forever. But now I know that death is nothing but a kind of sleep, and that those who sleep with their fathers, will one day rise again."

"He has uprooted the sapling and spared the gnarled old tree. He has cut down the bud, but left the wilted flower standing. His curse rests upon me and my house."

"No, Scipio, do not think that. Did the child not suffer but little pain? Were the eyes of his memory not clouded, so that his spirit could find peace? Did he not die with peace in his heart? How would you have felt if he had lived and had known everything? Is it not possible that it was the hand of love that took him away? Look, even now he is still smiling!"

"Woman, it is easy for you to speak such words. Your son, so you say, is alive at this very moment, and will once again delight your eyes. But my son is dead. His eyes will never again behold the sun, and his voice will never again brighten this house of desolation with music. They have left to prepare a place for him. They will lay his body in the grave, and I will never see him again."

"Scipio," she said, "your torpid heart is a dark veil between you and all truth and beauty. Please listen to me, while we are standing here in the presence of the seeming death. Thirty-three years ago a child was born in a stable in Bethlehem. I was the spouse of Joseph, a carpenter from Nazareth, but he had not yet known me as a husband knows his wife. The prophets predicted that I would bear a child, conceived of the Holy Spirit.

"A group of shepherds, of whom one is staying with me at this moment, will be able to tell you how the angels announced the birth of the child. The child grew up and became strong, learning Joseph's trade. He was not like other people – much of his sayings I did not understand.

"One day, when John the Baptist was baptising people in the River Jordan, Jesus went there, and John announced him: 'Behold, the Lamb of God!' John baptised him, and while he was standing in the water of the Jordan, a voice came down from heaven, saying, 'This is My Son, whom I love; with Him I am well pleased.' There are many people who are still alive today who will attest to the truth of all these things. The rest you know; how he died on the cross that day, at three o'clock in the afternoon. And on this first day of the week, in keeping with the prophecies and according to his own promise, he has risen from the dead."

"Oh, dear woman!" I said. "It is easy for you to speak these words, for your son who was crucified lives, as you tell me, but my little boy is dead."

"I am glad," Mary said, "that you speak from your heart, for truth lives only in the heart. Look! I will tell you something known only by a few. My son will only be seen for a short while by the eyes of the people. He returned only to manifest the power of the Almighty to us. He was the messenger of God. And now that he has finished proclaiming the message, and has manifested the power of God by his resurrection, he will ascend to the Father.

"It may well be that I will continue to live on this earth for some time after his departure, but I will not be without consolation, for he has promised to send his Spirit out among the people. In this love I will abide, until I am called to lay down the flesh. Then my liberated soul will be with him for all eternity. Did Hermas not leave behind his gentle spirit here with you, Scipio, and with Susanna, and with all of you? Prepare yourself, so that your soul, when it leaves your body, may be free enough to ascend to the higher spheres where God and your little boy live. Truly, I tell you, souls that are burdened by sin and doubt can never rise above the shackles of this earth. There is a dividing wall which souls that are bound to the earth cannot transcend. This I know, for he who has been raised from the dead has said, 'Blessed are the pure in heart, for they will see God.'

"Divest your heart of all sinful doubt and disbelief, and know that even though you are grieving for your loss now, the hour will come when you will see his countenance – perhaps in that paradise of which you heard the Crucified speak in the hour of his passing."

With these words she departed. To this day I can still see those tearful eyes and hear those tender words. And yet I did not know what to think, because I was speechless with grief and heard her words only as if in a dream. All I knew was that my beloved Hermas was dead and that my heart was lonely and empty. I could no longer stand being in that house of death. I got up and left the child to go to the tower. But I had barely stepped over the threshold before I again yearned to be in that quiet room. Nevertheless I continued. When I walked through the courtyard, I saw the sparrows that the child usually fed.

"You made a poor job of it, Scipio," said one of the soldiers of the garrison who was sitting by the gate, gambling. "The Galilean that you had left for dead has escaped from the tomb." He cast the die again. "Confound it, Publius. Yours again!"

I said nothing and simply walked on. If he had spoken to me in this way earlier, he would certainly have regretted it. Quintus was waiting for me at the door of the workshop.

"Licinius was just here," he said. "He has heard about everything that has happened and has granted you leave of absence so that you may bury your son. There isn't a great deal of work. I'll be able to do all of it by myself." I stood there before him like someone unable to comprehend anything. I saw him looking at my hair.

"Comrade," he said, and put his hand on my shoulder, "my heart is bleeding for you. Farewell!" He turned around and went into the workshop. I heard him, who was always so quiet and friendly, talking to the slaves in an uncharacteristically harsh way.

I went back to my own home, where I found Rufus and Probus waiting for me. They were tired and heavy-eyed, for they had spent the entire night guarding the tomb of the Crucified. In spite of this, they came to my house immediately afterwards to find out how Hermas was, and to tell me about the wonderful things that had happened.

Susanna, who had already returned, led our little procession into the death-room, where the two men bade the child farewell. Probus took off his helmet and leaned over the small body, with tears running down his weathered cheeks.

"Farewell, Hermas!" he said. He who once raised his hand to you, today grieves for you."

Rufus said nothing, but I realised that his sorrow was no less than that of Probus. He had always loved the child as if he were his own. I knew that he was secretly saddened by the fact the Deborah had never been able to give him a son. For a long time he stared at the little white face of the departed. The he lifted his eyes and looked at the mother with an expression that cannot be described in words.

"Come in here," Susanna said, as she left the room. We followed her and sat down in the room next door. For a few moments no one spoke a single word. Then Rufus said, "Scipio, tell us truthfully: do you know for certain and without any doubt that Jesus of Nazareth was dead when you took him down from the cross?"

"Rufus, would I who have gazed upon the countenance of death so many times not recognise it upon sight? Did I not guard the body with the greatest care after Licinius had spoken to me? Had Giron not driven his spear deep into the bare side of the man – yes, right into the heart, so that there could be no doubt? And didn't you yourself see the blood and water flowing from the wound? Why, then, do you ask such meaningless questions?"

"No, Scipio, I know very well that he is dead. But I am confused, because our eyes have witnessed wonderful things this past night, things that no man born of a woman has ever witnessed before. Listen, Scipio! You should know, and your wife Susanna too, that Probus and I have just come from Caiaphas, and he has immediately started to spread the rumour that the disciples have stolen the body of the Nazarene, because the tomb is empty. And yet no one touched the body; and we who were standing guard had not fallen asleep, for as you yourself know, Scipio, if we had, neither of us would have been here now. But he who was dead and lying in that tomb, has risen. I do not know what to think of it, but I am filled with fear. I think we killed a greater person on Golgotha than we knew."

"Look here, Rufus," I said. "During our wanderings and travels you and I have seen the temples of Apollo, Dionysus, Hercules, Mitra, Adonis, Osiris and many others. And you know very well that many Roman, Greek and Egyptian gods were supposedly born from a virgin. Likewise, it is said of many of them that they died and were resurrected from the dead. Are the stories told of the Nazarene not of the same nature as these stories? And Rufus, amidst all this confusion of faith, where do you think we will ever find the truth?"

Then Rufus looked at me, and his eyes were filled with sorrow when he said, "Forgive me, Scipio, if I say that your understanding is as murky as the dungeons of Antonia. Because of your disbelief you are greatly removed from the kingdom of truth. Concerning the gods that you have mentioned, we have heard nothing but legends and superstitious tales, and perhaps even lies. This Messiah – did we not see him ourselves? And did your own kin not hear and see his wonderful words and deeds among the people? Not one of the gods that you have mentioned has ever said such remarkable things as Jesus did. '*I am the way and the truth and the life. No one comes to the Father except through me.*' And upon further questioning he answered: '*Believe me when I say that I am in the Father and the Father is in me.*'

"It seems to me that the Truth was crucified on Golgotha, and that this same Truth rose from the darkness of death on the third day. You saw this Messiah hanging on the cross for three hours. Your eyes have seen and your ears have heard. And what is more, Probus and I have seen wonders in the heavens above and on the earth here below. We both saw the seal of the Sanhedrin on the tomb, and we both stared with our own eyes into the tomb that is now open and empty. And if you still doubt, can you doubt the change that has come over Probus and I – and, yes, also over those that you love? In vain we Romans brought libations, offers and sacrifices of atonement to our gods, because those prayers and sacrifices did us no good. But have not the good deeds of this Messiah been manifested to us in our loved ones? Indeed we judge a tree by the fruit that it bears."

But no word passed over my lips. I simply lowered my head and remained silent. Then Susanna said, "But this resurrection – how did it happen? Please tell us everything."

Then Rufus looked at Probus. "You tell them, Probus," he said. "You were there with me."

"No," Probus replied, "I would like to be the one to tell the tale, but I am not well-spoken. You should tell what we have seen, and I will bear witness to the truth of it all."

Rufus took a sip of wine and then started talking. "Licinius had ordered me to take a detachment of the garrison and to stand guard at the tomb in the garden of Joseph. I took Probus and Gregorius and Miles and Gaulterus and a few others and went to the tomb. Probus and I went to look at the tomb, and saw that there was a large stone rolled before the entrance, sealed with the seals of the Sanhedrin. I was convinced that no mortal being would be able to roll away that stone by himself."

"Yes!" said Probus. "But it wasn't an ordinary mortal that we were guarding. It was someone immeasurably greater. When he was standing there in the courthouse against the pillar I was angered by the fact that he would not cower in pain, and I swore that I would make him scream for mercy. But when he looked at me, the strength disappeared from my arm, and the whip that I held in my hand fell to the ground. His eyes looked right through me, and all the rotten fruits of my life lay spread out before him. And yet I knew that he did not despise me. No, he was filled with compassion. Even though he said no word, his lips moved; his eyes were raised heavenward, and it seemed to me as though he was praying. At that moment I knew that he was more than a mere human being, and that the welts on his back were like welts on the back of God himself.

He lowered his head, and for a few moments there was silence. "Go on, Rufus," he eventually continued (and his voice was nothing like the voice of the Probus that I knew). "Tell them about everything that happened there."

"Well," Rufus said, "Probus and I went back to the detachment, but we were disturbed by their constant blasphemy and did not want to be in their company. They thought that it was folly that they had to guard the tomb, while their comrades were drinking wine with the women of the city. So we got up and together we walked along the numerous paths in the garden. I don't know what it is, Scipio, but there is something in that garden of the graves that I have never encountered anywhere else. The night was calm and the sky was filled with stars. Everything was quiet, except for the soft whispers among the olive trees, as if the small, lost breaths of the wind were speaking of things that no man was supposed to know. The flowers filled the night air with a wonderful fragrance, and the moon cast a white glow over everything. A wonderful sense of peace took possession of us, and we conversed with each other as never before.

"It was already deep into the night when we went back to our comrades. They were very tired, but they were not asleep. They were leaning against the garden wall close to the wild fig tree, talking to one another in hushed tones. We returned to the tomb, about twenty paces from there. Pale and cold it lay there in the light of the moon. No one had touched the seals; everything was exactly as we had left it. However, we found the presence of the tomb too grisly, and we resumed our stroll along the lonely paths. It was almost sunrise, the time when everything appears vague and strange and dim. An unearthly light touched every growing plant in the garden. A soft rustling could be heard from among the blossoms of the orange trees, as if the world was waking up and starting to move in the dawn.

"'Look there,' Probus suddenly said, and pointed to the tomb. Listen, Scipio, that same tomb was enveloped in a silvery mist, and yet it was not completely silver, because a soft reddish glow was radiating from the mist, just as the rays of the rising sun clear a way through the silvery haze that lies upon the sea in the early morning. However, no sun has ever made its appearance in such glory. While we were looking, the mist started moving and reshaped itself into a number of wreaths around the tomb, so that it was obscured from our sight. The light changed to a deeper red, and started pulsing like a heartbeat through the haze, until every leaf and flower in the vicinity was tinted with a rose-coloured hue. Although everything was vague and dreamlike in that wonderful light, I thought I saw wonderful figures of the greatest beauty through the mist. They were human in form, and yet they were not children of this earth, for in their movements their feet did not touch the earth. And no man born of a woman possesses a radiance like theirs. I could, however, not see anything clearly, despite the fact that the light was shining ever brighter. I was afraid that I was delirious, and I therefore looked around me. I saw Probus beside me, and Gregorius, and the others beside the fig tree – they were all staring at the tomb with wide eyes. And I saw the leaves and the blossoms and the sleeping flowers, and the wonderful light shining on all of them.

"At that exact moment a bird started singing in the myrtle-tree, and suddenly it sounded as if all the birds in the whole of Judea joined in its song. Oh, music that did not come from bird or man, music more glorious than anything on earth, soothed our ears. And when the splendour of the beautiful sounds reached me, I suddenly remembered a passage from Scripture that I had heard from Deborah: '... *while the morning stars sang together and all the angels shouted for joy ...*'

"Scipio, that is what we heard: the stars were singing together and the angels were shouting for joy. I have heard many people singing together in Antioch, and I have heard great multitudes in Rome and in Athens, but all the singing of the earth is like a whisper in comparison to the singing of the morning stars. And when the angels took up the song, all the earth must surely have heard that song of joy floating down from heaven. Those grand tones rolled over Golgotha and were echoed by the city and by the faraway hills, until it felt as though the earth and the heavens were as one. And behold! When that awe-inspiring music tore open the skies, a light like that of a thousand suns burst from the sealed tomb. We fell to our knees before that blinding light, and for a time our eyes were like the eyes of the blind. Suddenly everything was quiet. The light from the tomb was extinguished, and nothing but a rosy glow remained.

"The stars paled in the morning light. And what a morning! Never before had the earth witnessed the equal of that morning. When the rising sun made its appearance above the hills, all the trees, shrubs and flowers adorned themselves in glorious hues of purple and gold. The air itself was pure joy – all sorrow and sighing disappeared. Scipio, that blinding radiance that no human eye could bear to look at was not the radiance of the sun, moon or stars; neither was it an earthly light. *I believe that it was the radiance of the glory of God!* And we, soldiers of Rome, were – as it were – struck with blindness before the majesty of that presence.

"Scipio! I have upon occasion heard you say that you could not see because the sun was shining in your eyes. Just like that we were lying there with our faces to the ground, covering our eyes from the light that blinded us. And I am telling you, in that moment, and in that glorious radiance, never before seen by any mortal eye, Jesus of Nazareth, the Son of God, stepped out of that tomb."

Rufus stopped talking and for a moment stared into space, like a man looking into the unknown.

"But tell me, Rufus," I said, "that stone (your speech is more like that of the poet than that of the solider; nevertheless, you are a sensible man and not someone who is susceptible to hallucinations), could a strong man not perhaps have rolled away that stone by himself?"

Before Rufus could answer, Probus was on his feet and said heatedly, "The stone was lying two yards from the tomb, and there is no man alive who could have rolled that stone from the entrance to the tomb. Even if they had piled all the walls of Jerusalem before that tomb, and had put on top of that all the rocks that were split apart on Golgotha, that crucified man would still have split that tomb asunder. Do you think that there is a tomb that can contain an immortal God?"

He who had before done nothing but mock, now filled us with the greatest awe, and we did not know what to say. He felt our eyes upon him and lowered his head.

"No, do not stare at me like that," he said. "It is only three days since he trained his eyes on me there in the Praetorium, and in that moment I knew everything."

To me the change in Probus was just as miraculous as the tale of the opened tomb.

"And then, Rufus," I said, "what then?"

"Just this," he said. "I looked at Probus. In terror I grabbed hold of his arm. 'Come!' I said, and we went closer to the tomb. The two of us were there alone; all the others had fled the scene, for at sunrise their shift was finished. The tomb was quiet and empty, and there were no particular signs that someone had lain in it. We studied the soil at the entrance carefully to make sure that no one had gone into the tomb, but in our hearts we were convinced that the tomb was opened from the inside."

"And what did you see?"

"We saw the marks made by the sandals of many men. But the footprints all belonged to the soldiers of the guard. As you know, Scipio, our sandals are studded with iron, and no one can mistake the print made by the sandal of a Roman soldier. And these prints were all just between the tomb and the wild fig trees.

"Was that all?"

"There wasn't any print made by other sandals, but we did see something else."

"And what was that?"

"A set of footprints made by bare feet. We followed these footprints until we reached a place where the ground was damp and soft. Scipio! What do you think we saw?"

"No, I don't know."

"In the print of each foot, the mark of a wound was imprinted clearly and freshly in the clay, like the hole that a nail would have left. We followed the trail even further, past the palm trees until we reached the road that leads to the Jordan and to Galilee, but on that road we lost the trail. We returned to the garden along the same way we came, and in fear and trembling we stood looking at the footprints made by the pierced feet of the Crucified.

"We went to Licinius in great haste and told him about everything that had happened. Then he took us to Pilate, and we reported everything to him that we had experienced. The governor did not speak a single word while we were talking, but the fear in his eyes was clear to see.

"'Now it is over,' was all he said, and then he turned around and walked to the foyer. There he came to a halt and said, 'Go to the house of Caiaphas and tell him about this.' However, he did not look at us, and his voice was hoarse and strange. You know, Scipio, I think that Pilate is afraid of this Jesus.

"Licinius led us to the palace of Caiaphas, and we told him everything. He did not move a muscle while he listened to us. His thin lips were pursed into a tight little smile, but the colour of his face reminded one of the colour of scorched wood.

"Then he mocked us, and said that we were children and dreamers of dreams. He also said that we were probably sleeping instead of standing guard. When he realised that this kind of talk did nothing to help him, but only made us more adamant, he tried to entrap and confuse us with cross-questions. But nothing could cause us to waver in our testimony. He then took Licinius aside and softly whispered something in his ear, while waving his arms about in all kinds of strange gestures, all the while watching us from the corner of his eyes. Licinius spoke no word, but simply looked him in the eye unwaveringly. When Caiaphas had finished speaking, he said in a hushed tone, but clear enough for us to hear, 'Am I a son of Israel to sell the truth for something like that? I am a soldier and a Roman. May your gold and your despicable words perish with you, you obsequious priest!' For a moment Licinius glared at the priest as though he wanted to strike him down. Then he turned around and walked out. We followed him.

"'Listen here, you two,' he said when we stepped into the street, 'if someone comes to you and instructs you to say that you were sleeping, or that the body had been stolen, or something of the kind, then strike him on his filthy mouth. And if you take gold from Caiaphas and spread such rumours, you will surely die. But I know that you would never do something like that.' Then he ordered us to go home and rest until tomorrow, and we left him and came here."

Chapter 18

"The resurrection and the life"

While we listened to the tale Rufus and Probus told, Nidia was preparing the meal, for it was already close to midday. However, we ate little of the food, since we were deeply afflicted and full of sorrow. After the meal I once again sat down beside the lifeless little body of my son. The small dead hand tightly clutched the tiny manger and lamb. It was Probus's handiwork. I sat down on the bench, and while my eyes were resting on the pallid little face, wonderful visions and long-forgotten memories appeared before me, just as they do before the eyes of a mortally wounded soldier on the battlefield, so that I barely knew whether I was awake or sleeping.

The only thing that penetrated my consciousness, was the fact that the sun was already high and was casting a bright light into the room, and that the boy was lying there, sleeping, never to awake again. With aching, yearning eyes I looked at him, for I knew that they would soon come to take him away. There was a smile on his face, as if he were dreaming a beautiful dream. My eyes were dimmed with tears, because I was sure that I could see his chest moving up and down. "He is sleeping," I said as if in a daze. "He's just sleeping. Hermas! Wake up! Wake up, my little boy!" I reached out my hand and took hold of his. It did not move, but remained white and still and cold.

I felt a hand on my shoulder, and when I looked up I saw Rufus standing beside me. He sat down next to me and took my hand in his. For a long time we sat like that beside the deceased, without speaking.

"He is asleep," Rufus finally said. "He is in a very deep sleep, but he will awaken from it again. Upon hearing the sound of the voice, he will arise and rejoice, for the tomb has been opened."

"Oh, Rufus, I don't know. Mary and Susanna talk about a place far from here where we will live again, but I don't know. The prophets and gods of many countries have spoken of a future paradise, but to me all of this seems vague like the shadow of a dream. Tell me, will I hear his voice again? Will he still be a little child and call me Daddy? What can you tell me of these things?"

"Listen, Scipio, I have not yet told you everything. Just as Probus knew when the whip fell from his hand, I have known since sunrise today. The sun rose over the hills of Judea; the flowers awoke; the birds sang. I covered my eyes, but the light was all around and inside of me. And when that voice so softly came to me on the morning breeze, saying, 'I am the Resurrection and the Life,' something that had been dead inside me for a long time stirred, awoke and was reborn. And then I *knew*. I opened my eyes. All of creation was a testimony to *life*. I knew that every wound would be healed, and that every tear would be dried. I knew that every setting sun would rise again. I knew that death was nothing but a passing dream, and that all sorrow and pain and loneliness would evaporate in the light of this joyful day. For truly, there is a hereafter that is prepared for us.

"Yes, Scipio, and what is more, even before I raised my eyes, I already knew that the tomb was empty, and that he who was asleep in it had risen." These were the words of Rufus. I was sitting beside him, but did not raise my eyes to look at him.

"The boy is dead," I said. "The boy is dead. Rufus, do you think that the Nazarene has the power to raise Hermas from the dead?"

"Certainly!" he said. "He has the power to do so, if he believes it to be for the best. But he has predicted days of famine, siege, plague, pestilence and desolation for Jerusalem. In this life there is enough sorrow, and very little joy. I doubt whether people will ever learn to live without fighting. Has the blood of innumerable armies not been shed inside and outside the walls of this city? If Hermas is not raised from the dead, he will never have to suffer all these things."

"How do you know these things?" I asked.

"I know it because I was told by Deborah, my wife, the one to whom the Nazarene granted forgiveness. From that day on, she has examined the Scriptures, and she delights in repeating the words of him who has forgiven her sins."

When he spoke of forgiveness, I stared intently at my right hand for a long time, but always and forever would I see the bloodstains. Rufus's hand was clean.

"Scipio," he continued, "you know how the Crucified suffered before he died and went to his Father, God. It may be that through loss and suffering we will recover the paradise that we have lost here. This miracle of the resurrection makes me think that death is nothing more than a darkened gateway to eternal life. Who knows, perhaps that cross that you erected on Golgotha will become a symbol of the cross that you and your loved ones have to bear. And not only you, but I too, and all of us, may carry in our hearts the cross as the Nazarene did. Who knows what the end may be?

"Today at sunrise I beheld with my own eyes the empty tomb, and this too may – before the end comes – become a symbol of hope for a world in misery. The Jews have sought signs and wonders, and truly, we have seen them this past night."

Rufus's face was radiant as he continued, "Such remarkable experiences have been our share these past days that I am completely astounded. Listen here, Scipio! Many years ago there lived in this land a great prophet, by the name of Isaiah. In his writings this prophet spoke of the Nazarene as a man of sorrows. Even then, in those long-past days, he prophesied this Scripture: *'In the future he will honour Galilee of the Gentiles, by the way of the sea, along the Jordan. The people walking in darkness have seen a great light.'* You and I have both lived among these Galileans, Scipio, but we never knew that from among them someone would rise to alleviate their darkness. Has this prophecy not also been fulfilled by the death and resurrection of the Galilean? You also witnessed the fulfilment of another of the prophecies on Golgotha. Did Gaulterus and Giron and the others not cast lots for the clothes of the Nazarene, after you refused to take possession of it? Well, listen to the words of this Isaiah: *'They divided my garments among themselves and cast lots for my clothing'*.

"There have always been innumerable astrologers, fortune-tellers, magicians and oracles. Many of them believe that our fortune can be read in the stars. Oh Scipio, now that our eyes have seen the truth, it does not behove us to speak of the stars. Instead we should speak of one star alone, the star in the east that the magi saw, the star of Bethlehem." Then he looked in the direction of the garden where the tomb was with a wistful expression in his eyes and said, "Scipio, do not ask me about the whys and wherefores of life and death, but go and ask him, for he alone is the Resurrection and the Life."

Rufus went out. I gazed at the calm, beautiful face of my son, and thought that I could see something of the peace and the serenity of the Nazarene in it, as I saw him that day standing before my lord Pilate. Yes, even now I can see him and feel his eyes upon me, in light or in darkness. Truly, those eyes transform night into day. When Hermas died, I felt something inside me also dying. Perhaps it was the evil that was in me. At that time I wondered whether this could explain the new and wonderful thoughts that I had. Was the spirit of the boy busy guiding me to discover a certain purpose in the confusion of this life? For the first time since the crucifixion, I took the bloodstained nails from my bag, and while looking at my hand, I repeated my oath there beside the body of my son. Once I had fulfilled that oath, I would seek out him who had risen from the dead. I would fall down at his feet and unburden my heart to him.

At about sundown Nidia came to me and said, "Father, there is someone here who wishes to speak to you."

I went into the other room, and found none other than Joseph of Arimathea. But he was not standing as tall and proud as he usually did. Instead, his head was bowed to his chest. I was astonished that someone like him would visit our humble little home.

"Are you the mother of that brave little Hermas who tried to save the prophet of Nazareth from the cross?" he asked Susanna. The mother nodded her head in silence. "Yes, my lord," she answered, "it is as you say."

"I would so much like to see the body of the boy," he said.

I took him to the room. There he stood for a while, looking at the smiling little face, softly shining like a sleeping lily in the dusky light. Then he turned to me. "You have probably heard that the Nazarene has risen and that the tomb is empty. To me that tomb is like the Holy of Holies. No one else has lain in it, and no one else will ever be buried in it until the end of time. But listen! There is another tomb in the garden, a tomb that was prepared for my own son, who, alas, perished in the water of the Great Sea. Look, I offer you this tomb. I do not come to ask for the body of the child, I come to offer you the tomb. The place is directly next to the holy tomb, and your son is worthy of it."

"Let it be so," Susanna said. "My lips cannot speak everything that is in my heart. Please accept the gratitude of a disconsolate mother, for I know that there the child will sleep in peace."

"My servants are waiting outside and are at your disposal," the rabbi said. "Please instruct them as to the arrangements you wish to make for the funeral. They will do your bidding. Peace be with you!" Then he turned to the bed once again. "And as for you, Hermas," he said, "you have found peace." And with these friendly words he took his leave.

Chapter 19

Joseph Gives a Funeral Oration

The day and hour had come for us to bury the child. Rufus, Probus, Caius and Quintus carried the bier. We left that cheerless house and went into the street, where a great crowd was waiting for us. They all followed us to the garden, for the news of the boy's death had spread very rapidly. In addition, there were strange rumours about the way that he had died. But I paid little attention to who was present there, or to what they said. I simply walked along with downcast eyes. "Whatever happens," I thought to myself, "the boy is dead."

We entered the garden through the same gate that they had carried the body of the Nazarene only three days before. The sun was shining, the scent of flowers filled the air, the birds were singing. "They are mocking us," I thought to myself, "because everything is alive, but he is dead." When we reached the tomb, the pallbearers put the body down below the cypress trees next to the entrance. Susanna and the women who had tended to the body of the Nazarene, now anointed the body of Hermas.

Nidia picked some flowers and placed them on the body. Then a boy brought a wreath of fragrant blossoms to her and said, "Look! I brought this for him. I am Samuel, the boy who fought with him at the temple. May I please place the wreath on him?"

Nidia nodded, and the boy placed the flowers on the still little chest. "Farewell, Hermas," he said, as he bent and touched the bier with a trembling hand. Then he lowered his head and sobbed with grief. Many of the bystanders could also not contain their tears. Everything was quiet except for the half-stifled sobs. Then the words of the Nazarene sprung to my mind: "The day will come when all nations and all tongues will gather around my broken body." Was this the beginning of the fulfilment of his prophecy?

When everything was ready Joseph lifted his hand. "Children of Jerusalem," he said, "please listen to me." I looked at him, filled with despondency, but the words that he then spoke still live inside of me to this very day. "Today I, that Joseph to whom the people have given the name of the Just and the Compassionate, want to speak to you about my own wickedness and indolence of heart. For I, who am so highly regarded by everyone, condemned a righteous man by my silence. And he who is lying before us now, a boy I did not know before this day, gave his life so that a righteous man should not die. I am not worthy to offer him a resting place. Yet listen, while I tell you why I wish to do so nonetheless.

"They brought Jesus of Nazareth before us, before the Sanhedrin. I knew that he was without sin, but my fear and my pride compelled me to keep my silence. They dragged him before Pilate, they flogged him, they took him to Golgotha. And that day I sought peace and rest in vain, for my soul was dejected. I went to the temple to pray, and behold! I was overwhelmed by a great fear, for the sun was eclipsed, the temple was cold and the air was damp. Then there was a bolt of lightning brighter than the sun at midday, and then darkness again. I fell down before the altar. And while I was lying there like a dead man, the thunderclaps followed one another in quick succession, until it felt as if the very heavens had been torn open. Storm and earthquake shook the foundations of the temple and the thick walls trembled and shook. In my unworthiness I called out, 'O great Jehovah, have mercy on me!' And then I heard a voice in my ear: 'Joseph, Joseph, what are you doing here? You who have awaited the coming of the Messiah for so many years did not know him when he made his appearance. And in the hour of his agony you withheld a helping hand?' And while I was lying there on my knees I heard the screaming of the hordes on Golgotha. The temple grew unusually dark.

"I looked at my hands. Had he not said, 'If your right hand causes you to sin, cut it off?' If I had had a sword with me, I would surely have cut my hand off there and then. 'Strike me, Lord!' I cried. 'Strike me down and kill me, for my sin is too great!'

"Then the voice spoke again: 'Your hour has not yet come; there is still much for you to do. You see here before you the temple curtain that covers the Holy of Holies. When this curtain is torn in two from top to bottom, the Holy of Holies will be revealed to the eyes of all people, so that all generations may see the beauty of sanctity through the life and death of him who is hanging there on the cross at this moment. And it will be the sign that he has given up his spirit. When you behold this, go to Pilate and ask him to give you the body of Jesus, and your request will be granted. Then immediately take the body and put it in your own tomb, so that the prophecy may be fulfilled: *"And they gave him his grave with the godless; and with the rich man he was in his death."* Let it be known to you now that he will rise again on the third day.'

"I did as the voice instructed me to do. I ensured that the body of Jesus was laid in the tomb, and behold! On the third day he arose, as many of you, who are present here today, can attest.

"He has conquered death and snatched the victory from the grave. It has been revealed to us that no earthly tomb could contain someone who came to illuminate the world with his miraculous glory. Even though it is very late, a little gleam of the truth is starting to penetrate our minds. We expected a king, and behold, one did come, humble and gentle of spirit and we did not know him. Now we realise that what we thought was wisdom has failed us. We have learnt that truth is not only revealed to the human mind, but to the *heart.*

"The poor people of Galilee, men and women of simple faith, met someone who wandered beside the sea and walked through their wheat fields – a man of humble descent. And yet, these people recognised him as a king. Perhaps it will always be so that proud and self-satisfied people will not see him, and that only those with a repentant spirit, those who are humble in nature, and those who are broken-hearted, will find in him a comforter and a saviour. The shame of this I will bear: that I, who so long expected the coming of the Messiah, feared and doubted. And while I denied and betrayed him by my silence, someone else, the child of a Roman, saw in him the Holy One of God and sacrificed his life for him.

"That is why I give to this child the tomb that I have hewn from the stone for my late son Rhesa, as an acknowledgement that my sin is still before me and so that my heart may be purified. And those of you who love this child, listen to me. I do not want you to grieve like those who have no hope. For will he who broke the seal of death not gather the soul of this child who loved him so much in his arms?

"Until that time, dear Hermas the Brave, sleep on. You are the first, perhaps of many, to lay down your life for Jesus – the Christ – the Holy One of the Almighty.

"As for you, Susanna, grieving and downcast mother, the Nazarene might perhaps still create a heaven in your broken heart, because you know that he has turned death into nothing more than a sacred sleep. And when your son awakes, may it be in the paradise that your faith promises you."

Then he spoke the final words of the burial ceremony, and we bowed our heads. We kneeled and said farewell to the child. Then Susanna said to Mary, "Mother of the Holy One, your presence has sanctified the grave of Hermas. If you had not visited us amidst your own sorrow and revealed the glory of your son to us, this day would have been eternal darkness to us."

"Look!" Mary said. "Look how, even now, he is smiling in his sleep."

Then the women arose and carried the body into the tomb. The sun was setting in reddish hues over the hills of Ajalon as we returned home from the garden of the graves. With despondent hearts we set out on our journey back. I looked at the setting sun and did not care whether it would ever rise for me again. And my heart was callous and my thoughts bitter, when Susanna took my hand and whispered in my ear, "Scipio, you are too dejected. I wish you could hear the voice speaking in me at this moment saying: 'Mother, do not fear. Look, I live.'

"Oh Scipio! In my heart I know that all is well with the child. In the days of famine to come, he will not want for anything. No sorrow nor pain awaits him. We who have stayed behind will taste death, perhaps only when the years have turned us old and grey. But he passed away in the light of the dawn. Old age will never wear him out. His foot will never falter and his eyes will never grow dim. The years will not weaken him, for time carves no furrows in the brow of eternity."

Much more she said, but I paid no heed to her words. I lowered my head and walked on in silence. The moon was rising and night was upon us before we arrived home. At the threshold I came to a halt. I simply could not enter that gloomy house where I would certainly miss his childish laughter and amusements. Without a word I turned around and I would have disappeared into the darkness had Susanna not taken me by the arm to restrain me. I broke loose from her, for I was afraid that I would behave like a woman, and I did not want her to see my tears.

I left the city and wandered into the deeper silence of the open fields. And still his voice sounded in my ears: "Daddy! Daddy!" It said thousands of little things that I had paid no heed to before. I did not know where my feet took me, but when I looked up I saw the hill of the crucifixion lying white in the moonlight, and I was standing before the tomb in which the child lay. A powerful longing to see the face of the Crucified – the Resurrected – once again took hold of me. And yet my heart was beating fast and loudly, for I was very afraid. I cast myself down before the tomb.

"Hermas!" I cried. "Hermas! My son, my son!" Again my heart was hardened towards this Jesus. My entire body was trembling, and I wept like a child. When I finally opened my eyes again, the stars were already fading in the sky. My body was damp with dew.

I got up and returned to the lonely house, without seeing him.

The days that followed were like the shadow of a dark cloud upon me, for my heart was despondent. Nothing brought me pleasure. Susanna had taken ill. It was, I thought, truly miraculous that her strength had not already given out before the funeral of Hermas. She had been overwrought the night when she returned from the house at the Sheep Gate – the night when they took the Galilean prisoner. The following morning the one that she worshipped was crucified, and her son was brought to her, mortally injured. For three days she watched over the child without closing an eye. In addition she patiently tolerated my actions. Without tears she witnessed them carrying him into the tomb, and she tried to console me, while I thought of nothing but my own grief. And when the child was no longer there, she lay down on her bed and closed her eyes like someone who was exhausted to the point of death.

The doctor came and examined her. "She is completely overwrought," he said. "Her spirit yearns for rest."

"Is it serious?" I asked.

He looked at her again and shook his head. "No, I don't know. But who can tell? It appears to me that this illness is more a matter of the heart than of the flesh. Let her rest, and look after her with great care." And with that he left the house.

"The curse rests heavily upon me," I said to myself. "Blood demands blood."

My fellow soldiers at the fort said many strange things about me. Rumour had it that Scipio the Bull was demon-possessed, and that the prophet had placed a curse on him. The hair on my head was no longer dark; the burdens of so many years had overcome me in one single night. I no longer participated in the jokes and the singing of the team, and the dice, the fencing and the discus no longer gave me any joy. I sat by myself, away from the rest, and drank more than usual. Only Rufus and Probus dared to speak to me.

In the evening I sometimes visited the grave of Hermas, or else I sat alone in my room, listening to the women talking next door.

Mary the mother, and Joanna and Deborah, and the wife of Cleopas, and some of the other followers of the Nazarene took turns to keep watch over Susanna.

They often fell silent when I came into the room where they were sitting, but I never spoke a single word to them. I sat in the shadows without moving, so that they forgot their fear and started talking to one another again without restraint. I heard many wonderful things about the Nazarene. I heard how he had appeared to some of his disciples several times – yes, one by the name of Thomas had even put his hand into the wound in Jesus' side, so they said. Others met him near the town of Emmaus, but did not recognise him until he broke bread with them. It also appeared that he never stayed long, always disappearing after a short while, but no one knew where to. Caiaphas and other influential priests never left their houses during the daytime, because they were afraid of meeting him in the streets. All these things I heard, and many more, but I listened like someone who understands nothing. "Oh, if only the boy was here with me!" was all I ever thought.

Susanna was lying there, so exhausted that she might very well die, but to my shame I could not scrape together the courage to speak words of comfort to her. She often asked the women to tell her about the Nazarene, and she never tired of hearing these tales. But there were times when she was delirious, and then she said strange things. Sometimes she imagined that she was standing outside Gethsemane and that she wanted to warn him who was inside that there were people who wanted to take his life. At other times she called out, "Hermas! Hermas! My son, where are you?" and then she moved her hands about as if she expected to touch him, sitting there right beside her. Again she kept a vigil by his bed, while death slowly made its approach; or she stood beside the tomb while his body was laid inside. But never did I give the slightest indication that I had heard anything.

"He has no heart," they said. But when the women were not there, I could find no rest. I sat down at the window and stared into the dark night, my thoughts preoccupied with the things that had happened. The new day usually found me in that position.

I was sitting there at the window one night, when I heard someone sliding open the bolts. I looked up, and saw Nidia leaving the house, looking fearfully around her. She had not even gone twenty paces before I caught up with her. Her eyes were filled with fear and she cringed from my touch.

"Where are you going?" I asked.

"I am going to look for Jesus, so that he can lay his hands upon mother and make her well."

"Is that so? Then you wish to bring the Crucified here to my house, to the one who, who ..."

"Father, you are afraid. I have never seen you afraid of anything on this earth. Then why are you afraid now? Is the life of your Susanna not worth more to you than your shame?"

But I cursed her and chased her back to the house. I bolted the door. "Go to your room, child!" I said. I sat down at the window once again and looked at the stars, while listening to her sobbing, which continued deep into the night. Why I treated her so harshly I don't know. I did not doubt the power of the Nazarene, neither did I know whether I loved him or hated him. Perhaps I was afraid that he would take the life of my Susanna too. But I think I did this because I was afraid to look him in the eye again.

Chapter 20

Mary Magdalene speaks

The next morning Susanna was worse, and by the evening, she was just lying there, exhausted and feverish. And all the while she was calling for the child. The doctor came to see her again.

"Is there nothing you can do?" I asked.

"Very little, I fear," he said. "She has suffered a great deal. A woman is not like a man."

"Will she die?"

"I don't think so. I can find little wrong with her body. But before sunset tomorrow, you will know."

"And is there nothing that *I* can do?"

"Nothing, and yet everything. The potion I have given to Joanna to administer. But think about this: if her spirit can find peace, her flesh will also regain its strength." When he reached the doorway, he stopped and looked back. "Scipio Martialis, have you done anything to help her spirit find peace? Do you console her now in the hour of her greatest need?"

Eighty years had made his back bent and crooked, and his hands were weak and trembling, and yet I feared him when I looked at him. Then a sudden burst of rage almost caused me to choke. "What do you mean?" I called after him, and stormed to the door.

But he had already gone. I returned to my usual place in the shadows, and in my heart I said to myself, "The curse rests heavily upon me. Tonight she will die."

"Go and fetch the woman from Magdala," Mary, the mother, said, "for she is a very able nurse. She can also tell Susanna about the things that happened there in the garden, for news about the Messiah always brings rest to her soul."

And so they brought Mary to her.

"Look, Mother," Nidia said, "look who's here. It is Mary Magdalene, the one of whom the mother spoke yesterday evening."

"Are you the Mary," Susanna asked, "who went to the garden of the tomb to anoint the Christ?"

"Yes, it is I."

"Then please tell me everything that happened there."

"Listen, Susanna, and do not harden your heart towards me if I tell you that I was that wicked woman, Mary Magdalene, to whom he granted forgiveness and whose sinful heart he purified. And yet they arrested him. The feet that I had washed with my tears, they pierced with nails. The hands that he laid upon my head with so much love, they shattered; the heart that took pity upon me, they broke, while mine lived on, filled with sorrow. I would have preferred to die with him. That night of the Sabbath sleep deserted me; it was a night of the bitterest dread. The temple trumpets announced each passing hour, while my soul sorrowfully mulled over the same refrain: 'Crucified! Dead! Buried! Crucified! Dead! Buried! My Lord!'

"I vaguely recalled that he had spoken of his resurrection – how he would rise from the grave on the third day. However, even though I knew that he had raised Lazarus from the dead, and also the son of the widow of Nain, I simply could not think how anyone could raise himself from the dead. My fervent love for him had not cooled, but my hope for his kingdom, power and glory had disappeared. Time and again I fell to the floor in my room, struggling with my doubt and my fear. In fragmented form I repeated many of the wonderful words that he had spoken in Galilee and Bethany.

"I knew that I would love him until death closed my eyes. Perhaps I had not understood his message. He was dead, and yet his disciples had believed that he would never die. While it was still dark, I rose and went to Mary the mother, and to Joanna and a few others. Together we went to the garden of the tomb. 'Hasten ahead,' Joanna said as we stumbled along in the darkness, 'hasten ahead, for you are young. Perhaps you can find someone to help us move the stone from the entrance.'

"I ran ahead. And behold, I ran into a group of soldiers who were terrified and ran away from the tomb with the greatest haste. I asked them to come with me and help me remove the stone from the entrance, but they called to me, 'The stone has been flung away and the tomb is empty.' A great fear took possession of me, and I hurried along to the tomb. I saw no one else, except for two men from the legion, who were leaving just as I reached the garden.

"I came to the tomb, and it was as the soldiers had said: the stone had been rolled away and the tomb was empty. I ran back to the other women and told them what had happened, and then we all returned to the tomb together. And behold! At the entrance to the tomb someone was sitting, clothed in glorious, luminous white, so that we fell to our knees and covered our eyes. How long we were lying there, I do not know. Then he spoke to us and said, 'Why do you look for the living among the dead? He is not here; he has risen!' We hid our faces, for we did not know what to say. And when we looked up again, we were alone.

"The other women went to the city to look for Jesus, but I did not leave the garden. I do not know why I chose to stay there, but I did not want to leave the place where his body had lain. I walked to the palms that stood close to where the road to Galilee runs past the garden. My heart was filled with a joy that transcended all words. But while I was still revelling in this joy, the tempter came to me and said, 'Mary, your joy is in vain; this Jesus has not risen. They have removed his body and hidden it where no one will find it.' My joy suddenly became sadness, and I went to the small stream that irrigates the garden. In the words of our King David I prayed, 'O Lord, save my soul from false lips, from the deceitful tongue.' Then my strength was renewed and my hope restored. At the cool stream I quenched my thirst, and in the clear water I could see my eyes, red and swollen from crying. Through my falling tears I saw the anemones in flower, glowing red in the early light of the morning sun, yes, red – red like the blood of the Crucified.

"And behold, while I was sitting there, weeping beside the murmuring stream, I heard a voice say to me, 'Woman, why are you crying? Who is it you are looking for in this garden of death?' I looked up through my tears, and saw a man dressed in white. 'I cry because they have taken away my Lord, and I do not know where they have put him.' I put out my hands to him and said, 'Sir, if you have carried him away, tell me where you have put him, and I will take him away.'

"But one word he said. 'Mary,' he said softly and clearly. And I trembled, for I knew that the man standing before me was none other than Jesus – my Lord and my King. 'Rabboni!' I cried. 'Rabboni!' I fell to my knees before him, and wanted to kiss his feet, but with the greatest of tenderness he forbade me to do so.

"'Go to my brothers,' he said, 'and tell them that I am returning to my Father and to your Father.' Then he left me as though he was floating (for it appeared as if he was not touching the ground) and disappeared from my sight in the direction of the Jordan and the road that leads to Galilee."

This is the tale that Mary told. For a time there was silence, and then Susanna said, "Listen here, Mary, and tell me only one thing. I had a son, an only son, a boy of nine years, and now he is dead. I know that he will live again, for Jesus loved him very much. But do you think that I will once again see his face and touch his little hand? For now he is lying there in the cold darkness, in the place of decay. Will I see that same flesh again, and touch that same body that used to go everywhere with me? Tell me this, you who have seen the risen body."

Mary answered her and said, "Listen here, Susanna, and let me share with you what I heard this day from John, our beloved brother. This same John told me how he and Peter and James were with the Lord on Mount Tabor. There, before their very eyes, Jesus changed form, and his countenance became as radiant as the sun. His clothes were white like pure light, so that no man could look at him. I think something of this kind must have taken place before he left the tomb. It was most assuredly the body of Jesus that I saw, because the holes made by the nails were in his feet and his hands, and on his forehead were the marks left by the thorns. His body was the same body I had seen before, and yet – it was not the same. It was as if even his wounds had been exalted. There was a divine holiness over him, a majesty, which was not of this earth. What had been mortal had become immortal. Never again will he taste death.

"I wanted to touch him, but it would have been like touching that which does not belong to this earth. The ground upon which he stood was holy ground, sanctified by a spiritual presence of the most profound glory. Wreathed with light and immortality he passed through the palm grove, surrounded by the spirit of God. In Galilee I had seen God as man; at sunrise of that blessed day I, Mary of Magdala, saw *man as God.*

"I was there when they laid him in the tomb. And behold! From the unfathomable mystery of the grave he appeared in all glory. Death has been conquered, and the ramparts of the grave have been destroyed. He who was crucified, dead, and buried, has given us eternal life through his resurrection. Oh Susanna, do not fear. On that day when the graves surrender their dead, Hermas will rise. The body that you gave him will have been changed. Fatigue and old age, illness and decay will never reign over him; but a beauty like that of him who was resurrected will be his share eternally."

These words of comfort pleased Susanna's heart. It was late already, and the women rose and spoke a few words of blessing over our family. Then each of them departed to her own home.

For a time I remained sitting in the shadows. I had listened to the words of the woman from Magdala, but I had also been pondering the doctor's remark that I had done nothing so far to comfort Susanna. I rose and went to the bed. She laid her feverish hand in mine, but not a single word passed over her lips. And so, in silence, I sat with her until she fell asleep. Then I returned to my seat by the window and stared into the darkness, my thoughts upon the days of yore. My heart was heavy, and I longed for my son.

"My child! My child!" I cried in my sorrow. "Why did you leave me behind so lonely?" Then I felt an arm around my neck and heard a voice in my ear: "Father! Father!" I looked around, and saw Nidia standing behind me.

"What are you doing here?" I asked.

"Father, do you not have any other child?" With wide eyes I looked at her, but didn't understand what she meant.

"Father, I know that your heart is broken. I know that you loved Hermas, just as I love you, and I have so much wanted to console you, but I do not know how. Oh Father, it is so difficult to suffer alone. Can you not share your grief with me?" Still I stared at her as though I did not comprehend her words.

"Father, I know that you could never love anyone else as much as you loved Hermas, and neither do I ask that of you. But do you not love me at all?"

Her cry pierced my heart like a sword. I looked at her and realised that in my sorrow I had barely paid any attention to her. In fact, I had only spoken harshly to her or ignored her altogether. I remembered how she looked after Susanna and took care of me. And never, not once, had a word of reproach passed over her lips. For the first time I noticed that she looked pale and tired, and that there were dark circles under her eyes.

"Father, do you not love me at all?"

"My child, my child! Forgive me! Forgive me, I beseech you!" I cried, and hung my head in shame.

"No, Father, do not say things like that," and with these words she hesitantly stretched out her arms towards me. Then she pressed my head to her bosom, while kissing my hair.

"Oh Father, how often have I longed to do this. Many a time I came to the door without you knowing, and watched you while you stared into the dark night. My heart yearned to console you and to hold you like this, but I didn't dare. I could do nothing but return to my bed and lie there, crying. Father, you could never know how much I love you. And I thought that you didn't care."

She kissed me again and stroked my hair with her hand, something that immediately reminded me of Susanna. "Oh Nidia," I said, "you are your mother's daughter. And a greater compliment no one can pay you."

"Well, Father, at night when you are sad, we will sit by the window, the two of us. And we will talk about Hermas, and about the past, and I will console you."

She lifted my head and pressed her cheek to mine. It was warm and wet with her tears. "My little girl!" I said, as I put my arm around her. And so we sat there for a while. Her breathing became soft and light, and it wasn't long before she fell fast asleep. I picked her up in my arms and laid her on the bench. She stirred and opened her eyes. "Father, where are you going?"

"I am going to seek Jesus. Sleep in peace, my child. I left the house and walked into the night. By the time I returned, the eastern horizon was already pale with the first light of morning. I searched the entire night, but again I didn't find him.

When I came back from the garrison at around sunset that afternoon I felt someone touch my arm. It was Nidia. She was breathless and her eyes were sparkling with excitement. "Father!" she said. "Do not fear. Everything is well now!"

"Then your mother is better, and you have come to bring me the good news?"

"No, Father, I have not seen her since the midday meal, and then she was still very feverish. Listen, Father! I had heard the women say that Jesus was nearby Bethany. I therefore went there to fetch him. And truly, I saw Jesus and told him everything. 'Daughter,' he said, 'do not fear, but have faith, and your mother will be given back to you.' I then left there and came back here in all haste. When I reached the gate, I saw you and first came to you. Hurry, Father, and let us go to her."

And when we arrived home, we indeed found Susanna dressed and on her feet. She ate of the food that Nidia prepared for her, and from that day on her strength was restored. Her spirit was also not as distraught as before. That evening the three of us sat together in the little room, while Nidia told her mother everything that had happened in Bethany.

"Oh, how I wish that you could have seen him, both of you! When I went to him I was very fearful and did not know what to say. But when they brought me into his presence, and his eyes looked into mine, all my fear disappeared. Yes, and I knew that I loved him. What I said I do not remember, and I don't believe that I needed to say much, for when he looked at me I knew that nothing was hidden from him. He laid his hand on my brow and said, 'My child, you too have suffered, but only those who grieve can know your joy.'

"And Mother, then he told me that you would get well, and he instructed me to return home and to look after you. When he smiled at me like that, I could have kissed his wounded hand, for never before has there been a tenderness the likes of his."

"Listen here, Nidia! You spoke of a *wounded* hand. Did you see that wound?"

"Yes, Father, there was a wound in the palm of each hand."

"Tell me, did he say something about ... about me?"

"No, Father, not a single word. And yet it seemed to me that nothing was hidden from him. But oh, if only you could have seen him. Then you would have known that he has nothing but loving forgiveness for true repentance."

That night, after Nidia had gone to her room and Susanna was already asleep, I sat by the window for a while, staring into the night. But the bitter thoughts that had earlier tormented my spirit no longer troubled me, and peace like a sacred balm came upon me. Then I took the cursed nails from my bag and looked at them a while. His blood – the blood of the Christ – was like rust upon them. And I renewed my oath upon them. "This debt will be paid," I said, "and even if his blood must be upon my head, I pray that my wrongdoing will not be reckoned to those who come after me." Then I hid the evidence of the crime in a safe place and lay down on the bench. I immediately drifted into sleep and slept until sunrise.

Chapter 21

"If your right hand causes you to sin ..."

The following day I left the workshop earlier than usual and went to the woods of Ephraim. The sun was already low when I reached the spot where we had felled the tree from which to make the cross. I went to stand before the big stump which was still in the ground, because, from the moment I had sworn an oath on the nails, the words of Joseph the council member had been resounding in my ears: "He said, 'If your right hand causes you to sin, cut it off.'" If every tree in the woods of Ephraim had a tongue with which to address me, I could not have heard those words more clearly. What I cannot understand, is that I did not think of Susanna for a single moment, nor of the legion in which I would never handle the sword again.

I saw only one thing; the tomb containing the body of my only son. Another tomb appeared before my eyes, the tomb in which the compassionate lay, he of whom the people said, "He always put out his hand to heal and to bless." And mine? Oh, woe is me! It was my hand that drove the nails.

I pulled my sword from its sheath and laid my right hand on the stump. What I did, I did quickly, and before the sun had set, I had fulfilled my vow. I took out the roll of linen and all the other things that the army provided for the dressing of wounds on the battlefield. I had, in fact, gained a lot of knowledge on how to stop bleeding from old Simon the chemist. So I dressed my hand; the hand that had sinned would never sin again. I cut the flesh from the bones and hid the bones from all eyes.

(The rumour spread among the people that Scipio was mutilated while he was working; while others referred to it as a punishment for his sins, and perhaps they were nearer to the truth. In the garrison there were various rumours about the way I had lost my hand, but no one came close to the truth, except perhaps Rufus and Probus. I paid no heed to all the gossip, but the memory of what had happened in my own home will always remain fresh in my mind.)

After I had fulfilled my vow, I returned to Jerusalem, and although I had lost a lot of blood and had walked many miles, I was cheerful when I approached the walls of the city. Still, I didn't wish to be seen by anyone that night, because I was worried about Susanna. It was already very late, but when I opened the door to the room, they were waiting for me. I will never forget how pale Susanna turned as she came to me. She became as white as a leper. "Scipio, Scipio," she called with great concern in her voice, "you have been hurt! What happened to you?" But Nidia leaned over her and whispered something in her ear. Then Nidia came to me. "Let me help you, Father," she said. She tended and dressed my arm with a skill I did not know she had. Her tears streamed onto the linen cloths wrapped around my arm, and she looked at me with a tender intensity. Oh, the beauty of those eyes filled with love and compassion, yes, and a holy pride radiating through the tears. When I looked into those eyes, all my pain disappeared.

And from that moment neither Susanna nor Nidia ever asked me any questions about this matter, but both treated me with the greatest affection. And in their eyes I could see the light of understanding a man longs to see in the eyes of his loved ones. I therefore knew in my own heart that they understood everything, and why they did not ask any questions.

In the legion a soldier who mutilates himself is punished by death. I was not afraid for myself, but I feared that Susanna and

Nidia might suffer. When news of the matter reached the ears of Licinius, he came to me and ordered me to appear in the palace of the governor. To this day I do not know whether my lord Pilate or Licinius knew the truth about what I had done, but I wondered why neither of them asked me how or why my injury had happened.

To my surprise the governor, instead of handing down the sentence I deserved, offered to appoint me in his own household. Although many of the gossips of Jerusalem did not have a single kind word for the governor, I knew him as someone who would never allow any act of personal service to go unrewarded. I realised that the crucifixion of the Nazarene had brought about a profound change in the life of my lord Pilate. His voice was hoarse and serious when he returned my salute and said to me, "Scipio Martialis, I am terrified about what we have done, because, truly, I found no guilt in the Galilean. It might be that there will be no forgiveness for our wrongdoings, because I indeed tend to believe, along with the noble Procula and with Licinius, that we killed someone who was more than mortal. My servants tell me that he died like a hero and displayed as little fear then, as when he appeared before me in the courtroom." It seemed to me as though his voice was trembling as he said these words.

Around this time there were rumours in the city that Caiaphas, in his letters to Rome, had attempted to sow seeds of discord between the governor and Emperor Tiberius. Furthermore, he intended to bring about the banishment of the soldiers of the guard who refused to accept his bribes. Since I very much wanted to stay in Jerusalem, because the body of my son was buried there, and because I was afraid that my lord Pilate could be transferred, I was very much concerned at the thought of what the immediate future held for us.

But behold, as I was contemplating these things, Joseph of Arimathea came to me. After commenting on my mutilated arm with much compassion, he continued, "Scipio, it would appear to me that, since you can no longer handle your sword with your right hand, you may be dismissed from the Antonia Fortress. And since Reuben, my gardener, has grown old in my service, I would like to allow him to live out his days in rest and peace. Therefore I came here to ask you whether you would be willing to become supervisor and gardener of the garden of the graves. There is a house for you and your family in the corner of the garden."

"I thank you, Joseph the Compassionate," I replied. I cannot remember what more I said, but my lips refused to pronounce the things my heart felt.

And then, to my surprise, he said, "You need not feel embarrassed if I were to tell you that Nicodemus and I saw you kneeling at the tomb of the Nazarene the night of his burial.

"We thought it wise to guard it, since we had heard various rumours. We stayed there until the soldiers of Antonia and of the temple guard arrived, and we were witnesses to the sealing of the tomb. If you were ever tempted to believe the lie that the body was stolen, I would like to give you my assurance now that from the moment he was laid in the tomb, the place was guarded closely."

Although I was embarrassed that someone had seen me in the garden, it was a great pleasure to me to know that the conspiracy of the Sanhedrin would be thwarted. And so it came about that I, Scipio Martialis, would enter the service of that righteous man from Arimathea, with the slaves of his household at my disposal to do the work I could not manage with one hand.

Susanna and Nidia were overjoyed when they heard that we would live near the grave of Hermas – yes, and near that other grave which had become holy ground to them, as it had to me.

Chapter 22

The snake has struck

Around this time something happened that caused great excitement among the soldiers of the garrison, and which also had the tongues of the Jews in Jerusalem wagging, although they only spoke about it in secret because they were afraid of the high priest. Caiaphas and his friends spread the rumour that the disciples of the Resurrected had stolen his body. (When I heard about this, I realised that the Arimathean had acted wisely indeed.) They tried to bribe Licinius again, as well as Rufus and Probus, but without success. Gaulterus, Miles and others took Caiaphas's gold and spoke as he instructed them.

"You just wait," Caiaphas said to Licinius when one day by chance they ran into each other near his palace, "you just wait. One of these days you will be sorry. The day is near."

It was about six days after what had happened in the woods of Ephraim that I was summoned by Licinius and went to his home.

"Farewell, Scipio," he said. "But there is something I have to tell you before we part ways."

"But, sir, where are you going?"

"I am going to Gaul."

"Is the detachment not accompanying you?"

"No."

"But why are you leaving then, sir?"

"Because the snake has struck. He did not kill, but the poison burns like fire. Listen to me Scipio, Pilate himself is afraid of this Caiaphas."

And then he told me how the high priest had conspired to bring about his transfer, as well as that of Rufus and Probus, because they had refused to assist in spreading the lie about the body of the Nazarene. Licinius had to leave for Gaul, while Rufus and Probus were made guards of the dungeons of Antonia by order of Pilate.

"Now listen, Scipio, there is something I would like to tell you. Now that your arm has been mutilated, you will not be of much service to Rome anymore. I therefore award you honourable discharge from the legion." And with that he handed me the paper of my release.

"Go and call Probus and Rufus," he said. "We will enjoy dinner together before I leave."

In the quarters of the centurion we sat down together at the table, the four of us: Licinius, Rufus, Probus and I. We did not eat much, but began talking about the days of old and about the many battlefields where Licinius had led us to victory.

"Yes," Rufus said, "they will never find another centurion like you again."

"And never will I find soldiers the likes of you again," Licinius said. "Do you remember the day we fought against the Nomads at the fortress of Machaerus? No one wavered. You, Rufus, took the sword wound that was meant for me; and you, Probus, stood fighting over me when I had been struck down. By the god of war, that was some day! And Scipio, will I ever forget the day when the spies brought tidings that Barabbas and his band of robbers had established themselves in the mountains near Jericho? Do you remember how we advanced on them, foot soldiers, cavalry and chariots? The leader of the robbers had to be arrested for rioting and murder. He had many followers, and all of them were strong fellows, while their leader was a veritable Goliath, fearless and extremely cunning.

"Do you remember how we defeated the band of robbers in a bloody battle, and how Probus pulled this Barabbas from his horse after a struggle? Then he fled into the ravines where no horse could follow him. And, Scipio, then you went in pursuit with incredible agility for someone your size – you ran among the rocks with the firm tread of a mountain goat. You overtook him, and when he turned around to defend his life and freedom, we heard the sound of the swords striking each other. Before anyone else could reach you, you had already disarmed your opponent with a mighty blow and had flung his sword through the air.

"With a roar like that of a wild animal in the arena, he sprang at you. Had he attacked anyone other than Scipio, the Bull, in this manner, he would have torn his opponent limb from limb. But, while we were anxiously watching the fight, it did not appear as though you had the least bit of fear. As swift as an arrow your arms shot out and grabbed him, and before we knew what was happening, you had grabbed this Barabbas with the skill of a wrestler and flung him over your head. We heard the thud as the body hit the ground, and we knew that it would be a miracle if a single bone in his body was unbroken. When I told this to my lord Pilate, he laughed and said that he had seen you handle a robber in a similar manner. Alas! Scipio, now those days are over, and even the robber Barabbas has converted from his evil ways – and now I am leaving."

He lowered his head and we all fell silent. Then he spoke again, but as if he was oblivious of our presence. "Quintus is now the centurion. He will do well. No one will be able to say anything against Quintus. Pilate chose him. Yet, it will never be the same again." Then he pulled himself together and looked around him. "Come," he said like one in a dream, "it is late. Before the sun sets I have to be outside the gates. I am no longer centurion here!"

We got up and followed him. He walked like someone who was very tired, and it looked as if the years weighed heavily upon him. But when we reached the gate we saw a strange sight, because Quintus had lined up all the soldiers of the garrison at the gate. In silence they waited there for us, and we had no choice but to pass through the lines. When we were close, Quintus gave the command, and each soldier saluted. Then I saw how Licinius pulled himself together. With a firm tread and head held high, he marched on as if he was once again leading his army into battle. He did not look to the left or to the right. But I, following close behind him, could hear how he drew in his breath sharply. Without a word we marched on, each looking straight ahead. We passed through the gate, and behind us a murmur could be heard that sounded almost like sobbing.

Then Licinius turned and answered the salute. He mounted his horse and joined those waiting for him outside the gate. With sad eyes we watched as he set out on the way to the Great Sea, until he disappeared in the distance. No soldier had ever known a greater and worthier centurion. Some of us felt that he had sealed his fate at the cross on Golgotha, when he called out in the presence of Caiaphas, "Truly, this man was the Son of God!"

Chapter 23

Scipio leaves the legion

And now I write about the wonderful thing that happened in the garden of the graves before we moved into our new home. I went there at midday a few days after Nidia had been in Bethany. For a time I sat there by the graves and thought about the two who lay there. It was a scorching day, and the sun was extremely bright. I went in deeper among the trees to find more shade, when I suddenly heard a voice calling me. I looked everywhere around me, but could not see anyone.

"Scipio," the voice said, "Scipio, do not be afraid. It is I." And then I knew. It was the voice of the one I had nailed to the cross. I fell to the ground, trembling.

"Fear not, because I did not come to judge, but to look for what is lost. Oh, foolish man! How little you knew me! You hardened your heart against me; you hated me, and yet I loved you. And although you sought me, your soul rebelled against me. Behold! I have been with you for a long time, but because of your lack of faith you were not aware of my presence. When you called for me that night of death, I heard your calls. When you laid down the bodies of the two who were crucified with me, I was with you. When Hermas, your son, closed his eyes in the sleep people call death, I was close to you. Throughout the night of despair and in the morning of bitterness, when you ate of the bread of loneliness and drank of the cup of sorrow, I was by your side. My heart was filled with compassion for you, and I longed to comfort you. And when you went to the woods of Ephraim, I was there also. I watched your deed, and I knew that you did it out of love for me, but you didn't know that I desire no other sacrifice than a repentant heart.

"Listen! Soon I will depart from this place to that paradise where your son lives now. Scipio Martialis, do you love me? Because I so much wish to take good tidings to your son!"

Thus the voice spoke and when I heard these words, I knew that my soul had finally found peace. I fell to the ground and cried, "Jesus, Jesus of Nazareth! You, who opened the eyes of the blind Bartimaeus, have opened the eyes of my mind with Your compassionate love. From now on I want to follow You, yes, until the very end."

I do not know how long I lay there, but a great peace, as I had never known before, filled me, and my heart rejoiced. Then I looked up in the direction of the Mount of Olives, as if something commanded me to do so. And behold, I saw a large group of people standing on the summit; and although I was at the tomb in the garden, it was as if I was taken to them in spirit, because I saw the Galilean women and the disciples who had followed him. And Bartimaeus was there, as well as the one they called the shepherd. The Resurrected stood in their midst, and he lifted his hands in blessing and his eyes were upon me. And while I was watching, a great cloud descended and took him away, and the heavens opened up and received him. And oh! There beyond the cloud I saw my son Hermas, clothed in indescribable glory. I only saw him for one fleeting moment; then the cloud ascended and covered the face of heaven.

Time had sped past while I lay on my face in the garden, and when I finally got up, the setting sun covered the hills with a divine glow. While I was listening to the songs of the birds in the trees, it appeared to me as if his presence had sanctified the earth. With this new peace in my heart I returned home. My tread was light and my heart was filled with joy, because I, Scipio Martialis, had witnessed the glory of God with my own eyes.

When I arrived home, Probus, Rufus and Deborah were there.

"Scipio!" Susanna called when she saw me. "Listen to this wonderful tale Deborah has just told us."

We sat down at the table, and while we ate the evening meal, Deborah repeated her story for my benefit.

"Scipio, today I have seen a wonderful sight. But I hardly know how to talk about it, because I fear you may find it too extraordinary to believe. But Peter and John and Bartimaeus and many others can attest that I am telling the truth. I heard that Jesus was near Bethany. I hurried there, and at the house of Lazarus I found a number of friends. Mary, the mother, and Mary Magdalene, and Joanna, and Isaac, and many others. But none of them had seen Jesus since sunrise. 'He instructed me to wait here for him,' John said. 'He will soon be here with us.'

"At about the sixth hour we saw Jesus approaching on the road from Jerusalem. He was alone. He greeted us with words of peace, and then he ordered us to follow him. 'I am going to the Mount of Olives,' he said, 'and on this day your eyes will witness the glory of God.'

"When we arrived there, he made us sit on the ground and spoke words of comfort to us. It was as if his eyes rested on the hill of Golgotha and on the garden of the graves with sadness. Then he looked at heaven for a few moments. Finally he got up and stretched his hands over us in blessing. 'Farewell, my brothers,' he said. 'I leave you my peace. It is better for you that I go to my Father; but I will not leave you without comfort. My spirit will be with you. Yes, I will always be with you until the very end of the age.'

"Then Isaac from Bethlehem – the same man who tried to save Jesus on Golgotha – threw himself to the ground and called, 'Lord, take me with You from here.'

"Jesus did not answer him, but only bowed down and touched him. And while we were watching, a great cloud overshadowed us, and we were filled with wonder. Then the cloud ascended, and Jesus was no longer with us. 'Look!' Peter said with his eyes directed towards heaven, and he pointed to the cloud. And there we saw Jesus in the middle of the cloud with his arms spread out, just as when he had blessed us. And before our eyes the heavens opened up to receive him, and he disappeared from our sight. Full of wonder we looked at one another. Then Bartimaeus went to Isaac and touched him. 'Get up!' he said, but there was no movement. Then John approached him and looked at him closely. 'The Lord has answered his prayer,' he said. 'He is with the Lord at this very moment.' Then we got up and came to Jerusalem.

"Scipio, what is the matter? You look like someone who is about to lose his mind."

"Woman, tell me this: When the cloud took him away and he ascended to heaven, didn't you see anyone else waiting there for him?"

"No, because the cloud hid him from our eyes. Why do you ask?"

"Listen! Just as you, Probus, knew the moment when the whip fell from your hand; and Rufus, just as you knew when the voice spoke at daybreak; so I too know now." And then I told them everything that had happened to me in the garden. They listened to me with surprise, just as I had listened to Deborah's wonderful tale. For what I had taken to be a dream that his love had held up to comfort my broken heart, was indeed a vision of what had actually occurred. Then Susanna rose and put her arms around me. "Oh, my love," she said, "now my heart rejoices. I have prayed for so long that you would learn to love him." And Nidia pressed her cheek to mine, and Rufus and Probus embraced me.

I got up and raised my right arm. "Listen!" I said. "Here before all of you I swear this solemn oath. You are my witnesses. I swear by the severed hand that drove the nails; I swear by the nails that were driven in! From this moment onward, neither the gods of Rome nor any other gods will rule over me. Today at the tomb I heard the voice of Jesus – Jesus of Nazareth, who is now, and will always be, the only true and living God. I will serve and worship only him. And I further swear this: those who love him, I will love; those who hate him, will be my enemies. My life and my strength, my body and my blood will belong to him, and he may do with it as he pleases, until the very end."

"And mine too," Probus said.

"And mine," Rufus whispered. And in turn they repeated the words of the oath. "Is there nothing," Probus wanted to know, "that we can do in his memory, so that the oath can be sealed?" We looked at each other in silence. Then Nidia said, "There is a prayer mother taught me, a prayer he gave to his disciples. Do you want to say it after me?"

"Yes," Probus said, and "Yes," we all replied.

"Say the words, my child," Susanna said, "and we will repeat them after you."

She raised her sweet voice, and we repeated the words she spoke out loud: "Our Father in heaven ..."

"Our Father in heaven ..."

"... hallowed be Your name ..."

"... hallowed be Your name ..." and so on until the last word of the prayer.

That night, while Jerusalem slept, I heard a soft knock. I rose to open the door, and to my surprise Archipus, the trusty slave of my lord Pilate, was standing there. He looked around carefully and held his finger to his lips. I gestured that he should come in, and he gave me a parchment with the seal of the governor. The document is lying here next to me as I am writing. And these are the words that were written there:

Pilate, governor of Jerusalem, to Scipio Martialis, greetings.

It appears that you were wise when you chose to join the household of Joseph the councilman.

I have considered your words carefully, and I can understand why you would like to pursue your desire to remain close to the grave of your son, the son whose noble deed led him to lay down his life.

By this time you would already have received, from Centurion Licinius, the documents containing the report of your services to the Roman Empire, together with your discharge from the legion, given under my seal.

You have always served me faithfully, and if you ever need anything, you only have to speak the word, because I will never forget that you saved me from the hands of a murderous band of criminals at grave risk to yourself.

I granted the wish of your two friends, Rufus and Probus, and as prison guards of the Antonia Fortress, they will no longer be involved in the execution of criminals on the cross. As for Licinius, I considered it to be in his best interests to send him to Gaul.

The hour has arrived for me to share with you what you have not known until now. Years ago I promised your father, Marcus Martialis, that I would keep an eye on you if you were to serve under my command. he was a citizen whom I held in such high esteem that the oath was never any burden to me. It is more than astonishing that you had to be the one to save me when the robbers attacked me.

Now I have heard from Licinius, the centurion, that it troubles you greatly that you had to be the one to crucify the man above whose head I posted the inscription: 'King of the Jews.' he says that you are going about like someone upon whose head the curse of blood rests. Yet, you only did what you were ordered to do as a soldier in the legion of Tiberius. The guilt is not on your head, but on mine, because I, as governor of Judea, succumbed to the demands of these Jews.

Two days ago I encountered Rabbi Joseph, and he told me how he, together with another member of the Sanhedrin, namely Nicodemus, had guarded the tomb from the moment that you saw to its closing, until the seal of the Sanhedrin was put upon it.

Early on the third day, when the tomb was open, those two saw the broken seal, and they maintain that, judging from the seal and the way in which the stone was rolled clear, without leaving a track on the ground, these things were not brought about by mortal hands.

I secretly visited the tomb, and I was surprised at the great weight of the stone that sealed its entrance. It is the greatest foolishness for anyone to claim that the body was stolen. And yet my view on the resurrection has, until now, been the same as that of the Sadducees. But if this Galilean truly rose from the dead, then he must be the first among those who sleep the sleep of death.

They say that many people have seen him. I can only pray that I will never encounter him on my way. These things are a mystery to me, perhaps a greater mystery than this world of ours has ever known. One thing I know for certain, namely that the pale face of the convict, as he stood bound before the judgement seat, will remain before me forever.

The rabbi's garden is beautiful, and you should find peace there: a peace that I, alas, can never hope to find. Do not forget what I tell you here, because the promise I made to your father must not be broken.

Well, I pray that the gods may bless your days. Should I write gods ... or God? Because it may be that you may find the only true God in this crucified Nazarene.

— *Governor Pilate* —

Now I understood for the first time why my lord Pilate had been so kind to me, for I had been unaware of any promise that was made in connection with me. I sat thinking for a long time. My thoughts were confused. I did not desire to leave the service of my lord Pilate, but some said that he would not stay in Jerusalem much longer. In any case, I no longer wished to place my sword under the command of anyone else. But it did me good that my lord spoke of me in such a kind manner. Also, I was grateful that the fact that I was entering the service of the rabbi did not displease him.

Chapter 24

The hero of the mountain

One evening towards sunset, Rufus and I were in Joseph's garden, and while we were sitting there, Centurion Quintus came to us. He was in a great hurry, and as he was approaching, he called, "Scipio! Rufus! Listen carefully! I have something very important to tell you. I have just heard that a mob of the temple guard under the command of Abdiel the Zealous, have gone to the wilderness of En-gedi in the Kidron Valley to look for the followers of the Nazarene. I fear that a lot of blood will flow.

"Because I know, my friends, that some of your loved ones are among the followers of this man, I came to inform you about this. You may still be in time to save them. I found Probus at the tower. He has already left for Kidron, but I fear for him, because his eyes were fiery. He is only one against many. You must hurry, or it will all be in vain. Don't tell anyone that I informed you of this."

"The Kidron Valley!" Rufus said. "They always meet in the cave by the gorge. Come, Scipio, that is where we have to go."

I didn't hesitate, but I had difficulty strapping on my sword (which I thought I had lain down forever); although I was pleased at the strength I still had. While I was struggling with the buckle, I thought of the words, "As we forgive our debtors." Yet, I did not hesitate for a moment, because Probus, whom I loved, had gone to do battle with those who dared to lift their hands against the Galilean.

Fear gave wings to our feet. Nonetheless, at sunset we were still a good three miles away from the place. We increased the pace, because some of our own family members were among those who went to that cave to worship.

"But you know the place, Scipio," Rufus said, "the secret place in the gorge, known only to the initiates of the holy sign. Somebody must have betrayed them, or perhaps Caiaphas's spies have discovered the place. Oh, Deborah, Deborah! I wish I were by your side!"

For a while we hurried along in silence, apart from the sound of panting breath, our racing hearts, and the snapping twigs. We made our way through the brushwood as only strong men filled with profound dread can do. The night was extremely dark; the moon was obscured behind the clouds, and many times we stumbled on the uneven ground and tore our clothes on the thorn bushes. How Rufus managed to lead me through it all, I do not know. I only know that we staggered along the rocky slope of the hill, and that the sound of the stream sounded far below in the gorge, and that a man was stumbling on ahead of me like a devil on the rampage, while he constantly called out the name of his wife, Deborah. It appeared to me as if the day would break before we would reach the secret path. And then suddenly we came to a halt before the great rock that obstructed the path. In our haste we had entirely forgotten about this obstacle.

"Come, Scipio," Rufus said, and his voice sounded hoarse and strange. "The two of us will have to push this thing out of the way."

Yet it was believed in the brotherhood that the rock could only be moved by the strength of many hands. We bent our backs for the task.

"Deborah!" Rufus called like someone in the utmost of despair; while my thoughts were once again occupied with the priests and my heart filled with a glowing rage. "Now!" I called and leaned against the rock with all my might. I thought my limbs would tear apart. In the darkness I heard Rufus groan. Slowly the rock moved. "Again!" I said. And it moved a little further. "Once more!" We pushed with the last blind attempt of despair. The rock trembled, wavered a moment, and then plunged forward and rushed down the slope in leaps and bounds until it reached the bottom. It appeared as if the entire rockface was being torn away in a torrent of stones and gravel. And then, with a tremendous crash, it came to rest in the depths of the gorge. The echoes had not yet disappeared when we resumed our race against time.

"Quiet," Rufus said suddenly. "I hear the sound of people walking."

We waited. A black shape sneaked past us in the dark and two yellow eyes glared at us viciously, then disappeared. The footsteps approached, and then the murmur of many voices could be heard.

"Who goes there?" Rufus asked, jumping forward.

"Who are you?" the reply came, and my heart lifted, because I recognised the voice of Peter, the brave protector of those who love the Nazarene.

"It is Rufus and Scipio!" I called out. "The mob of Caiaphas are at your heels, hurry up!"

"Probus told us in the secret cave. We are fleeing at this very moment," the disciple said.

"Probus!" I called. "Probus! Where are you?" for in my heart a fierce resolve was taking shape. There was no reply. "Probus! Probus!" various voices called, but no one answered, because he was not with them. No one had seen him since they had left the cave.

"Come, Rufus!" I said. "To the bridge! You and I can hold out against a legion."

Deborah was in his arms and clung to him, weeping. He embraced her. "Farewell, my love," I heard him say.

"May the Lord be with you!" she said. They tore themselves away from each other, and the two of us hurried to the cave.

If we can reach the bridge before the soldiers of the temple guard get there," I said, "then we will be able to hold out, you and I. And even if we die, we will still be able to hold them back long enough to allow Peter to lead the others to a safe place."

Rufus did not say a word, but stormed ahead like a man possessed. When we arrived on top of the hill, Rufus suddenly cried out – the cry of someone who had received a fatal blow: "Too late! Too late!" He stumbled against me and tore out his hair. "Too late! Too late!" he cried again.

For there at the bridge across the gorge we could see the glint of the weapons of a large band of men. While I was looking, I saw someone running across the bridge, and a shout rose from the band. The light of a torch reflected on the blade of a sword; the sound of steel against steel could be heard, and then a bloodcurdling yell split the air. For one fleeting moment I saw a man wavering on the edge of the bridge, with his arms aloft. Once again that terrible yell sounded in our ears. I heard something plunge into the gorge, and when I looked again, the shape with the outstretched arms was no longer there. But I saw someone else standing there with his head thrown back and a sword in his hand. In the strange light he had a supernatural appearance.

"Probus!" I shouted. "Probus! Do you see him, Rufus? Probus is defending the crossing!"

Rufus lifted his head and became a man again. With a violent bellow he lunged forward and stormed down the hill. I followed him. We watched them as we were approaching. Another attempted to cross the bridge; another yell ... and the defender was once again alone on the bridge. But only for a moment, because he was attacked by two more. One moment we saw the flickering circle of light, and men swaying from side to side on the narrow bridge. Then another body disappeared into the gorge while his cry of despair resounded against the cliffs. Two struggling forms were locked in a deadly battle; then the one rose up and stumbled aside while the other rolled over and fell into the gorge.

A wild cry of victory rose from the band on the opposite side, because the defender on the bridge had been wounded. His arm was hanging limply by his side. But their cries of victory died in their throats, because at the moment when everything appeared lost, we stormed at them, shouting. "Romani! Romani!" they cried.

"The Romans are upon us!" and then they turned around and fled. We were fortunate, for in their haste they thought that an entire band of soldiers from Antonia was attacking them.

I gave Probus, who had collapsed onto the ground, perhaps mortally wounded, only one look, and in my anger I ran in pursuit of the enemy, almost oblivious to what I was doing. All I could think of was that Probus had been wounded – Probus whom I had hated at first, and whom I now loved like a brother. Not for a single moment did I slow my pace, until I heard a shout behind me. I hurried back, and found Rufus engaged in a violent struggle with Abdiel the Zealous, the leader of the temple guard. The struggle was intense, and the bridge was covered in blood; if a foot were to slip, their bones would be bleaching in the gorge.

The Hebrew was gravely wounded, but he fought bravely and skilfully. Once Rufus stumbled, and I thought the fight was over. The end came suddenly. Abdiel fell forward, and his sword slid from his hand. Rufus held back his blow and gestured to him that he should pick up his sword. "Never!" Abdiel shouted. "Never from you, you heathen dog!" He rose and spat on Rufus. At that moment the light of a torch that had fallen on the ground revealed my presence, and when Abdiel saw that his chances were slim, he tried to escape. But just as he lunged forward, his feet slipped on the slippery surface of the bridge. With a cry of fear he disappeared into the gorge. We heard his body fall at the bottom of the gorge; then everything was quiet, apart from the shrieking nocturnal birds that were fighting over their prey at the bottom.

I went to the place where Probus lay. Someone was kneeling beside the body, and when I approached, I recognised John the disciple; and that other disciple, Peter, was with him.

"He is alive," John said. "Let us carry him to the cave." Rufus and Peter lifted the body of Probus. I heard the wounded man cry out, and I was afraid that the end was near. I walked ahead with the torch; John walked with me, because he knew the road well, and the path was difficult to find for someone who did not come there often. We were compelled to walk slowly and behind us we heard the wounded man moaning.

"Jesus! Jesus of Nazareth!" he called intermittently, and then he called the names of his comrades from the workshop. All the time Rufus spoke to him as a mother speaks with her child.

Then Probus shouted, "Hermas, Hermas my boy, have you forgiven me? Look what I have brought you!"

At that moment I once again saw a vision of Probus at the sickbed of the boy, and how tenderly he spoke to him. My eyes filled with tears.

Then John spoke to me and said, "We are now close to the cave of worship. Tonight you Romans have saved the lives of the followers of Jesus."

Then I remembered what had happened in the secret path. "Are they safe?" I asked.

"Yes. We went up to the place of the big rock, and behold, the rock was no longer there. Then Peter and I turned back to see whether you did not perhaps need us. This is the place. Rest here while I go to fetch a few torches."

We took Probus to the deepest cave and laid him down at the crack on the north side. By the light of the torch Peter and Rufus dressed his wounds, which, alas, were many as well as grave. They did not have much knowledge, and I wished that Atilius were with us; yet we knew in our hearts that no doctor would have been able to save him. After a while the moaning stopped. He closed his eyes and his breathing was heavy and laboured. We did not know whether he slept, or whether the fever made him delirious. Then he opened his eyes again, but we realised that he did not see anything. "Lavinia!" he called out. "Lavinia, where are you?" And then he thought that he was in the governor's palace with the whip in his hand. "No!" he called fearfully. "I cannot do it! I cannot! Because his eyes are on me," and he made a movement with his arm as if he was throwing down the whip. Then he closed his eyes with a smile. It looked as if he no longer experienced pain. A peace like that of paradise spread across his face, which had once been so brutal, and filled it with a wonderful and tender beauty.

"The end has arrived," John whispered. From a crack in the

rockface he took bread and a flask of wine. The cold sweat of death glistened on Probus's forehead. Once again he opened his eyes and looked at us while he tried to smile.

"I would like to administer the sacraments to him," John said. "It may not be known to you, soldiers of Rome, but before our Master went to Gethsemane, we, his disciples, met with him in a room in Jerusalem, and there our beloved Lord broke bread and gave it to us and said, 'This is my body given for you; do this in remembrance of me.' Then he also took the cup, and after he gave thanks, he gave it to us to drink from; and we drank while he spoke to us and said, 'I want you always to remember the holy covenant; the broken bread, symbol of my broken body. The cup is my blood of the covenant, which is poured out for many for the forgiveness of sins.'"

When John spoke these words, we noticed to our surprise that Probus heard and understood everything. First he looked at me, and then at Rufus, and finally he fixed his eyes on John, the disciple, with the words: "If you" – his voice trembled – "consider me and these comrades of mine worthy to participate in this covenant, then I request you to administer the sacrament to us."

"The time has come," John said. He took the bread, blessed it and then broke it, before giving it to us while he repeated the words of Jesus: "This is my body given for you."

In silence we ate the bread. Peter covered his face with his hands, and I saw tears running from between his fingers. John placed a piece of bread in Probus's mouth. Through eyes that were already dim with approaching death, the dying man looked at him earnestly. Then John took the flask of wine and poured some of it into the cup: "This cup is my blood of the covenant, which is poured out for many for the forgiveness of sins."

He drank from the cup, and then gave it to Peter, who tasted it and then passed it on to Rufus. In turn I was allowed to drink from the cup of remembrance. Then the disciple whom Jesus loved took the cup and leaned over the dying Probus. "Drink from the cup," he said, "in remembrance of Christ who died for you."

The shadow disappeared from the eyes of the dying man. With

seemingly inhuman strength he lifted himself onto his two feet and stood there for a moment, like a soldier about to salute. Then he took the cup and drank from it. As I was looking at him, I saw him direct his eyes to the opening of the cave, and a wonderful glow emanated from them. Then the cup fell from his fingers. He stretched out his trembling hands before him and said, "Look! he is calling me!"

He took one step in the direction of the entrance, and before we could reach him, he fell to the ground. Blood streamed from his mouth and mixed with the sacred wine on the floor of the cave.

Carried on the gentle evening breeze, the sound of the Levites' trumpets reached our ears, while we were burying the body of Probus underneath the overhanging cedars.

"Truly," John said, "he who had obeyed the commands of Tiberius in the past, has now heard the voice of someone infinitely greater. Look! He died in our stead!"

The body of Peter shook with a grief he could not suppress. He fell to his knees and sobbed out loud. As for me, I would have liked to have lain myself down next to the lifeless remains of Probus, a Roman who fought and died for the followers of the one who was crucified by us. All of us kneeled there, and then Rufus whispered in my ear, "I am convinced that the Nazarene was with him in the cave, because truly, a peace like that on the face of this dead man, I have never seen before. He truly did not die in vain."

"No," I said, "for I am convinced that the Nazarene has always been with Probus since the moment the whip fell from his hand."

Rufus turned his head away, because he wanted to hide his tears from me. The radiance we saw on the face of the disciple John, while he spoke in whispers of the day when the grave will surrender its dead, was not of this earth. And while we were kneeling there at the grave in the shadows of the cedars, this disciple comforted and encouraged us with trembling lips. "Because," he said, "your comrade will rise again."

It was almost daybreak when we despondently returned to the city along the paths of the goats, the city that was now even lonelier for us, because there was no longer a Probus.

To us the days of the legion were over. We moved into the home that the rabbi had prepared for us. Often, as was our custom, Rufus and I sat and spoke of the oath we had taken never again to pull our swords from their sheaths in anger, and how we had broken that oath. For hatred and anger had become our masters when we saw Probus standing there alone with lifted sword, fending off those who wanted to take the lives of the followers of Jesus. Perhaps true repentance would still find forgiveness with him who never spoke of violence, but only of love. He would understand that we could not have left Probus standing there alone.

The soldiers of the legion will remember him with pride, and honour him when they stand beneath the cedars at the grave in which a brother-in-arms had found his last resting place.

CHAPTER 25

TWENTY YEARS LATER

Twenty years have passed since the death of Probus. Yet, his name still lives among the survivors of those for whom he died. Rufus and Deborah now also belong to the household of the Rabbi Joseph. While Rufus tends the vineyard of the Arimathean, he revels in the thought that his days in the Antonia Fortress are over. Quintus has a position of power in Rome now, and in his letters he tells me a great deal about the Christians (because that is the name by which the followers of Jesus are known). Bartimaeus, already advanced in years, still visits us often. It is truly a wonder that he has survived the wrath of the priests, because his enthusiasm for the Nazarene often gets him into trouble. Truly, we are experiencing days of great danger.

My second son, Joseph Secundus (so called according to the wishes of the rabbi), to whom my wife gave birth the evening after Probus's death, has brought me a lot of comfort. This son of mine, Joseph, looks so much like his mother, Susanna, and it brings me great joy that he drank in the great love she has always had for the Nazarene along with his mother's milk.

Although the danger is great, he often goes with Susanna, Rufus and Deborah to worship in the gorges and caves where the followers of Jesus meet. Nidia is married to a man called Reuben the

Silversmith. They live in Jerusalem and also attend the secret meetings.

Because the rabbi is afraid that these writings may be placed in danger, he thought it wise that I not accompany them. Therefore they come home and tell me about the services.

My son works in the garden of the rabbi. He is very hardworking, and although he never knew Hermas, he always sees to it that his grave is kept neat. I have often seen him staring earnestly at the holy tomb for long stretches of time, and he always places the first and most beautiful flowers there. And now I realise that these writings must soon be placed in the wooden box that I have made for them, and I know in my heart that my son, Joseph, will honour the oath he has taken to guard and protect them, even with his life.

The night is near. I'm sitting here by myself, by the light of the lamp. It is time for the Jewish Passover again, and once again the moon shines brightly. Spring is here, the time when the birds sing and the voice of the turtledove can be heard in the fields. Tomorrow at daybreak I will go to the tomb, as I have done for the past twenty years, in remembrance of him who made this day holy for so many people.

Twenty years have passed since the streets of Jerusalem resounded with the call: "He has risen! ... he has risen!"

Oh yes! A daybreak to remember for all eternity. The daybreak when the soul of Hermas left us at sunrise. I walk to the open window, and my legs falter. It is strange, because my tread has always been firm and steady. I look at the sacred garden: the garden of the graves. Everything is quiet in the pale light of the moon. Green leaves are already appearing on the tender branches of the cypress trees. The lovely fragrance of the flowers fills the air and wafts towards me at the window. The silence is broken only by the rustling of the leaves and the cooing of a turtledove in the orange orchard. Truly, this night looks just like the night Rufus and Probus spoke of – the night when they guarded the sealed tomb.

From my window I see the moon shining on the grave of

Hermas. And close by – as if made of silver in the night of peace – is the holy grave, the grave of the one we crucified, the one we now worship as the Resurrection and the Life.

The tomb remains empty, because Rabbi Joseph (now old and frail) will not allow another body to be laid there. Susanna and my son Joseph have gone to the secret cave to worship. I hope they will return safely. I am glad that we could partake of the holy sacraments in his remembrance before they left. The beloved disciple John administered the sacraments to us.

A strange fatigue has come over me, fatigue as I have never known before. It might be that the end is approaching. And if this is to mean the last trumpet call for me, the last farewell to this fleeting and transitory world, then I must now – before it is too late, because my hands tremble and my legs are growing cold – I write down the name I once despised, the name that is now elevated high above all other names; the name that has become music to my ears; the last name I would like to mention before my departure ... Jesus ... Jesus of Nazareth.

Farewell,
Scipio Martialis.

It was during the Jewish Passover. My beloved father must have departed at daybreak. We found him in the garden, sitting on the stone that once lay before the holy tomb (the Rabbi Joseph never wanted the stone to be removed from the position in which it was found on the morning of the resurrection). He couldn't have been dead for long, because his body was still warm.

It seems that he went to put fresh flowers on the grave of my brother, Hermas. Then he must have strolled in the garden picking some of the most exceptional flowers. He had woven together these flowers in the shape of a crown – not a crown of thorns – no, a crown of the most beautiful flowers. The wreath hung from his right arm, the arm of which he had once sacrificed the hand. Perhaps that sacrifice was not pleasing to God, even if he did what he did, because of the anxiety of his remorse and out of love for the Crucified.

The fingers of the left hand clasped a pen, and on the ground beside his feet a piece of parchment lay, with these words written on it: "On this day, twenty years ago, Jesus of Nazareth rose from this grave."

He was probably going to fix this writing onto the crown of flowers, but death overcame him. Those were the last words my beloved father ever wrote. Although he was seventy years of age, it looked as if old age had been stripped away from him. There was a smile and an expression of tranquil beauty on his face. Perhaps Jesus had walked in the garden once again, and called my father in passing to follow him.

Joseph Secundus
Surviving son of Scipio Martialis.

Addendum by

Joseph of Arimathea

Since those in authority have of late taken it upon themselves to collect and destroy all documents and writings related to the life and blessed words of Jesus of Nazareth, and further, since a multitude of evil lies and atrocious, slanderous tales are spread daily about this same Jesus; I, Joseph of Arimathea, former member of the Sanhedrin, have undertaken to record the following.

It was around the ninth hour of the day on which Jesus of Nazareth was crucified, after I had handed Licinius, the centurion, a certain parchment with the seal of Pilate, that I encountered Scipio Martialis, a soldier in the legion of Rome, there on Golgotha – this very Scipio.

What happened in the garden and during the subsequent days can be read in the writings of Scipio. But I feel compelled to add something to it, because I know very well that there are many people who will doubt these writings and regard them with contempt – presuming that these writings will even escape the watchful eyes of the priests.

Scipio Martialis, a man of an exceptionally large build, a man with a fiery temperament and accustomed to war and blood from a very early age, now belongs to my household. Still, he has served me diligently and humbly for almost twenty years. And nowhere have I ever encountered a man with such a tender and compassionate, such a humble heart – with the exception of one, namely the one who was crucified.

Even now, as I write these words, I can see the Roman giant in the garden, busy weaving a wreath from select flowers to adorn the grave of him whom he loved more than life itself. And I lower my head in shame for the house of Israel. What Isaiah said is true: he came to his own, and his own people did not accept him.

What can I say about Susanna, the spouse of Scipio and a true daughter of Israel? Who can point a finger at her? Who has walked this humbly before the face of the Lord, impeccable in all his commandments and laws? And what more can I say about Nidia, except that Susanna lives in her?

The body of Hermas, the oldest son, who was glorified in death, lies in the tomb near the one in which the body of the Lord lay.

Joseph Secundus is standing by my side as I write this, a young man of strength and sincerity – a worthy follower of the Christ.

Now, concerning Scipio: a sense of shame and remorse has cast a dark shadow over his life, because he never held anyone else accountable for the death of Jesus, but took all the guilt upon himself. Thereupon he took an oath that he would put everything his eyes had seen and his ears had heard about the Christ into writing, from beginning to end.

But, for the sake of his son and his descendants, and because those in authority want to destroy all writings about Jesus of Nazareth, it would be imprudent to reveal everything now already. But on the day when these truths will be revealed, in case there are those who want to doubt the written word, I, Joseph the councilman, who knew Scipio Martialis well, and who knew about all these things from the beginning, attest that he recorded the things that his eyes had seen and his ears had heard, truthfully.

I would like to mention one more thing here. Many rumours have been spread about the death and resurrection of our Lord. Some claim that Jesus of Nazareth never tasted death, but that he went into a coma on the cross. Others proclaim the fallacy that his disciples stole the body. But I truly know that the man who was laid in the tomb was not alive, because the body was already cold as marble and there was no sign of life.

The whip had unravelled the silver thread, the spear had shattered the golden vase, and the precious lifeblood had been poured out. Yes, until the third day, no one touched the tomb, except those who sealed it. I swear this, because Nicodemus and I guarded the tomb without anyone knowing.

Yes, I know for certain that Jesus Christ was crucified and died, and that he was buried under those cypress trees. I know that death had no hold over someone like him, for on the third day at sunrise the bonds were broken; the tomb opened, and he appeared clothed in shimmering radiance. I know now that death is not an eternal sleep, for on that day when the graves will surrender their dead, I will rise and stand before him; and in my mortal body I will see God; I, Joseph, who despised and loathed him and who did not know him, will see him and be known by him.

Truly, Moses said, "Every matter may be established by the testimony of two or three witnesses." Therefore I chose Nicodemus, a rabbi of Israel, to attest to the truth together with me.

Amen.

Joseph of Arimathea
Nicodemus Ben Gorian
(Signatures on the original manuscript.)